A BABY MIGHT BE CRYING

A BABY MIGHT BE CRYING

by

Margaret Thomson Davis

Allison & Busby
published by W. H. Allen & Co. Plc

To my sons *Kenneth Baillie Davis*
and *Calvin Royce Davis* with much love

An Allison & Busby book
Published by
W. H. Allen & Co. Plc
44 Hill Street
London W1X 8LB

First published in Great Britain
by Allison & Busby 1973

Reprinted February 1988

Printed and bound in Great Britain by
Adlard & Son Ltd, The Garden City Press
Letchworth, Herts

ISBN 0 85031 094 6

Chapter One

Excitement crowded the Glasgow air like fast-bouncing footballs. Flags rippled and crackled. Everywhere the Scottish lion cocked up on its haunches, paws sparring. Headlines boasted:

EMPIRE EXHIBITION—1938

Alec Jackson felt on top of the world. Head and shoulders above everyone else he swaggered along Springburn Road, whistling through mobile lips well practised in exploring women as well as sound.

He winked in passing at a huge fat wife with a wispy black moustache and a head spiky with curlers.

"Hello there, gorgeous!"

The woman squealed with laughter then bawled after him:

"Wait till I get my hands on you!"

He twisted round without slowing his pace and bulged his eyes in mock shock.

"Sex maniac!"

Then, still without bothering to look where he was going, he swung into the dark close at the corner of Springburn Road and Wellfield Street.

"Oops!" The pram he had bumped into creaked with the weight of three children and was pushed by a grey ghost. "You don't need to use force, gorgeous. I'm all yours!"

"Alec!" The ghost changed with a smile, tightened, brightened, became a self-conscious, coy young girl. "What a fright you gave me. You shot in the close like a bullet. Do you never take your time?"

He pinched her bottom as he passed to go clattering up the stone stairs.

"I would with you, love."

He stopped on the first landing, his fist raised to rat-tat-tat at the middle door, when he remembered that the Hunters had moved from their single-end to a room and kitchen on the top flat.

He took the other two flights three steps at a time and reaching the top attacked the door with a good loud thumping.

It opened in a couple of minutes and he followed Ruth Hunter to the left of the shoe-box hall and into the kitchen, his eyes never leaving the undulating flesh beneath her pink sweater and red skirt.

"Two shillings, is it?" she appealed, lifting her handbag from a chair and easing a softly rounded hand inside it.

"You can have it for nothing from me any day, gorgeous!"

One eyebrow arched up as she slid a look that cut him down with sarcastic disapproval, yet the sexual awareness still remained.

He snapped open his brief-case, tossed his book on to the table and thumbed through the pages.

Sammy Hunter was a lucky man. He could imagine Ruth pestering him for it, pleading with him every night.

With one hand Ruth slid a two-shilling piece across the table, with the other she guided her insurance book towards him. He marked up the book with a flourish.

"I like your new place." Alec gazed around the kitchen as he tucked his pen into his pocket, and gave himself a pat. "You and Sammy certainly have good taste."

She forgot her sexy performance for a minute. Enthusiasm and childish eagerness rushed to take its place.

"You really think so?"

"Of course I do, love. Real high class, this place is. The pair of you have worked a miracle in here."

"Sammy did all the electrical work. He studied a book on how to do it. We did the painting and decorating between us."

"Good for you!"

"We had to get a plumber to shift the sink, though."

He looked over to the kitchen window where all the houses had their sinks, with pot cupboards underneath. In place of a sink, a sewing-machine stood in front of the window. Gold curtains were drawn back on either side and, on top of the machine, a vase of marigolds reflected the sun like glistening oranges.

"Shift the jaw-box?"

"Into the cupboard! Isn't it marvellous?"

Ruth knocked into a chair in her hurry to reach the cupboard door and two or three long strides took Alec over beside her to peer inside.

"What a bloody good idea!"

She flashed him a look and he apologised for the bloody, but she wasn't really annoyed. Sheer joyous pride swamped every other emotion.

"It's even got a light!"

The light clicked on, displaying Sammy's patient and conscientious workmanship of shelves and drawers fitted to the walls and under the sink. Alec could just see Sammy with a book in one hand and a screwdriver in the other. If he had managed a window that would have been something. Still, it was a bloody good idea.

"I like the colours." He grinned and nudged Ruth, immediately electrifying himself with the heat and the bouncy resilience of her flesh. "None of the old cream and green, eh?"

She shrank away but it was a graceful feminine movement. She had remembered sex again.

"I love pink and red. It's so nice and warm."

"Yeah!" Alec's groan of enthusiasm aimed straight for the bulging sweater and skirt. Pressing back against the sewing-machine, wriggling quickly then slowly as if she were squashed up against him, she shrank further away.

"Do you like it here?"

He gathered a kiss in his fingertips and flipped it to her.

Ruth brushed past him, the invitation in her eyes hooking him and pulling him along.

"The room's the best," she said and a pulse skittered through him.

The kitchen bed-recess had been made into a dining-area. That meant that the bed must be in the room. The room's the best, all right, thought Alec. Hallelujah!

Unexpectedly Ruth stopped and indicated a cabinet made of the same polished oak as the sewing-machine.

"That's the bed. The mattress folds up inside during the day."

Alec did not give up hope. He grinned cheekily down at her.

"I've heard of it happening in many a place but a cabinet's a new one on me, love."

The sarcastic look returned, sarcastic, yet sexy.

"You want to see the room?"

"I'm fascinated."

Across the small hallway she picked her way, high heels clicking on the linoleum, buttocks bunching and quivering.

He could imagine her as a sultan's favourite concubine, or a king's mistress at a French court, or a hot-blooded temptress of a belly dancer. A belly dancer—couldn't he just imagine that!

In the front room, she swivelled towards him, her breasts jiggling like jellies.

"Of course, it's not nearly finished yet. Still the bare boards, but look at the paper! It's the latest thing. We got it in town. And see the hole-in-the-wall bed?"

He lit a cigarette to help keep his hands off her.

"Eh? Where?"

Delighted again, a child-woman, she giggled and wiggled, and pointed to the wall where the bed-recess ought to have been.

4

"Behind there. We're using it as a store place. Sammy made the wall, imagine! It's wood, papered over. Listen!"

She tripped over to press herself against the wall and knock on it.

She looked good enough to eat.

"Fascinating!"

"Are you laughing at me?"

"I was thinking you look good enough to eat."

She struggled to cool her giggles, to flap superciliously at him with long thick lashes on a tip-tilted face.

"It's really too early to show it to anybody yet."

"Never mind." He grinned. "I'll be back."

She ignored his innuendoes.

"Have you got tickets for the Exhibition, by the way?"

"Sure. I've got a season. I'll be there at the opening ceremony with the King and Queen in Ibrox Stadium tomorrow. Will you and Sammy be there?"

"No, we're going straight to Bellahouston Park. Sammy hasn't much time for royalty or the military or the powers that be. Sammy's very independent minded."

"Me too, but it's the wife." He shook his head. "Anything for a peaceful life."

"There's going to be a march-past of all the services, isn't there? It's Sammy's father. You know what he's like, don't you?"

"Who doesn't?" He grinned. "If it wasn't for his gammy leg I bet he'd be marching along beside them, bawling the odds." He coarsened his voice to a snarl. "Left, right, left, right, left, left."

She shook her head and sighed as she opened the outside door but her eyes were smiling and her red mouth full and soft.

"Cheerio, Alec."

"Cheerio, love."

He savoured her all the way down the stairs and when he crossed the road outside he looked up at her front room window in the hope that she might be there to give him a wave. Her double window in the old tenement building sparkled with cleanliness and was edged with royal blue curtains. It looked like a precious jewel in a crumbling stone setting.

Ruth had been on his book nearly three years now, almost from the time she married Sammy and moved into the single-end at Springburn Road. She had been sweet sixteen then but every bit as lush as she was now. He reckoned that she must always have been sexy. Even as a two-year-old those eyes of hers would have had a coquettish twinkle.

He had missed out on those years because, apart from being quite a bit younger than Alec, Ruth was a Springburn girl and he had been born and brought up at Townhead. He had always been secretly proud of his origins, although he would tell people that Glasgow could sink in the Clyde for all he cared; and that he would rather have been from wealthy blue-blooded stock, with the emphasis on wealthy. The truth was that he was proud to be a true Glaswegian, with his roots in the oldest part of town. Glasgow had not originated down at the Saltmarket on the edge of the River Clyde as a lot of people imagined.

Years ago, as a wee laddie sheltering from the rain in the public library, Alec had discovered that St Mungo, the patron saint of Glasgow, had set up his monastery across the road, only a stone's throw from his own tenement building. St Mungo had chosen the very ground where Glasgow Cathedral now stood, grey and aloof yet not too far back from the crush and buzz of the Castle Street pavements, only separated by the small Cathedral Square, with its statue of King Billy on a horse with a broken tail that would wag in the wind.

From the Saltmarket at the river's edge to High Street and Castle Street then on to Springburn Road was practically a straight line on the map, right through Springburn to Bishopbriggs, once the bishop's riggs or fields.

Graduating from an infancy of tottering about his own

6

back-court and close, Alec had first explored the area immediately surrounding it. Against the skyline of the Necropolis across the road, all crowding together, stood the cathedral, the towering Royal Infirmary, Duke Street Prison and the Drygait where, according to the book, such great lords as the Dukes of Montrose had their town houses long before the prison dominated the place, a giant black castle of doom.

He had chuckled at the thought of lords living there because he knew the Drygait only as a slum.

Then on his own side of the street was Provand's Lordship, the oldest house in Glasgow, now a museum. King James II and King James IV of Scotland and Mary Queen of Scots were all supposed to have slept there.

As he got older Alec had wandered further afield down High Street to the Gallowgate and along to the Barrows, or right down by the Saltmarket to Glasgow Green and the river.

He didn't very often travel up the other end towards Springburn because at that time there never seemed to be anything of much interest there. Springburn Park was the only exception. It meant a really wild game of football, plenty of swings, a pond with paddle boats, and if you took a jar you could catch minnows.

Alec had seen Sammy there long before Ruth met him. The irony of it! Instead of bumping into Ruth, it had to be young Sammy. It would have been hard to miss him, of course, a red-haired, dour-faced unwilling conscript in his father's army.

Hodge Hunter, an ex-sergeant-major in the military police, marched his brood round the park every Sunday and then forced them all through a variety of physical jerks. Kids came from miles around to jeer at them and risk a fractured skull from Hodge's silver-topped stick.

If only he had hung around Springburn Road instead of the park! Alec cursed himself as he legged along the

7

road. If only he had lounged around the cafés, or the corners, he might have met Ruth before Sammy did.

But what was the use of worrying? The old shoulder-twitching bouncy swagger returned, and he was whistling cheerily by the time he turned right into Cowlairs Road, past a few closes and right turn again into Cowlairs Pend where he now lived.

His whistle bounced off the dark brick tunnel entrance of the Pend and reverberated back from all sides like noisy drumming with the clanging of two feet on the cobbles making a riotous accompaniment.

Emerging at the other end in the yard, with houses squashing in all round and the row of overflowing middens in the centre, he made a rush at a tin can and dribbled it across to the outside iron-railed staircase of Number Five. One last kick at the can before it was pounced on by a horde of howling footballers in short trousers and braces, some sporting shirts, some jerseys, some vests, others bare-chested.

Up the stone steps two at a time, his brie-fcase banging against the railings. Then into the close, a wooden-floored one that thumped hollow, past the bottom-flat doors, and up creaking wood stairs to his own right-hand door on the first landing.

The door stood open and Sheena the mongrel bitch lolloped out to meet him, tail a-wag.

"Down, girl! Get off!" He shied her away with his brief-case, rattling along the lobby littered with clothes pegs, pot lids and empty milk bottles.

Madge called from the kitchen:

"I'll murder Sadie and Agnes. They were supposed to pick them up."

She was sitting wide-legged by the kitchen range feeding Maisie. Maisie was nearly a year old and his mother said it was time she was off the breast but Madge just laughed.

"Och, what's the harm? If the bairn howls during the

night the breast's easier than getting up for drinks or to make bottles."

They had produced four children in their four years of marriage, the four-year-old twins, Sadie and Agnes, Hector who was three, and Maisie the youngest.

"Sadie!" Madge yelled in the direction of the kitchen door and the room beyond. "Agnes, come on, hen. Clear the place up for Daddy!"

Maisie sucked on regardless as Alex chucked her under her wet chin and fondled the heavy pendulous breast squashing against her busy pink cheeks.

"Get off," Madge told him automatically, but she raised her face to be kissed, a square, shiny face with fine white skin smudged with freckles. His lips fastened warmly and wetly over hers and his tongue was just beginning to weave from side to side and push further in when she suddenly broke away, big-mouthed with laughter.

"Sheena! My God, her nose is cold."

"Down, girl. Down!" Alec cuffed the dog's ears and its head bounced off Maisie who sucked on, ignoring it. "I'll just put my case away, Madge, then I'll run down to give MacVene my line."

"Hey, never mind giving the bookie your money. How about me? Remember you promised to take us to the Exhibition tomorrow. It's no use going without any money. Especially on the first day."

"Don't worry, you'll get the winnings—you big-breasted beauty you!"

"Get off!"

She punched him and tucked her short straight hair behind her ears.

"Tea's ready. Don't you be long."

Already he was whistling away to the room to put his case in his roll-top desk.

Sadie and Agnes were getting the bottles and the pegs from the lobby.

"Hello, sweethearts."

9

He put his hand up Sadie's skirt and tickled her, and on the way back he stopped to fondle Agnes, slipping his fingers inside her pants to feel the soft hot hairlessness of her, before whistling out of the house, across the yard and out of the Pend.

MacVene was the bookie's runner who hung around one of the closes further down Cowlairs Road and collected "lines" or bets for O'Hara the bookie, his ferret eyes all the time watching for the police.

Alec put sixpence each way on "Starter's Orders" and went to join the crowd of men lounging and bantering at the corner of Springburn Road. At this junction Cowlairs Road joined Springburn Road at one side and Vulcan Street joined it at the other to make Springburn Cross. Springburn Road had existed for hundreds of years and there had always been some hamlet or village round about the Cross. There had once been an inn, so the story went, and a burn which started as a spring, hence the name Springburn. The mind boggled at the idea of country inns and green grass, burns and springs in this place.

Alec hung a cigarette on his lip, rasped a match up to light it and wondered who would want Springburn to be like that anyway.

Springburn Park was there for the kids if they wanted it. He had enjoyed his occasional safaris there but he had always found it alien land. It was more up the hill in Balornock than in Springburn, and could only have got its name because one of the gates was at the Springburn end, at the top of the Balgray Hill. Or perhaps the park had been there, with its marvellous view of Springburn and the whole of Glasgow, long before the existence of Balornock.

No, give him old Springburn just as it was, any time any day, but especially right now with the hooters screaming and moaning and competing with each other for air space and the air stretching in the ears, alive, vibrating and painful with the racket. From all around Castle Street to the far end of Springburn men in dungarees and sweaty shirts and dirty faces were surging on to the streets in enormous black waves. Men were mobbing from the chemical works, the locomotive works, the iron works, the younger ones whooping, shoving, tripping, punching and bawling in the exhilaration of suddenly being let loose.

Springburn was a man's place and men converged on the Cross from all sides, and clanging tram-cars lined up in Springburn Road rocking with the weight of men.

Cowlairs Road led down to Cowlairs works, the head-quarters of the celebrated North British Railway Company's stud of bronze-green locomotives, now spewing out its men to mix at the Cross with the crush from the Hyde Park Works at the foot of Vulcan Street.

A tram-car ground and sizzled past from the town end and Alec caught sight of Sammy Hunter sitting at one of the windows, stockily built, in a navy suit and white-collared shirt, his thick hair spiking up from its brilliantine plastering, his bushy brows jutting aggressively forward.

Alec blew out a tight stream of smoke from a fluted tongue. His eyes were on Sammy but his thoughts had returned hot-footed to Ruth.

Chapter Two

In between serving customers at the general counter, Catriona kept glancing across the shop to the bakery side where her father-in-law was interviewing Mrs Jackson, a tall scraggy woman who had come about the cleaning job. Mr MacNair's brusqueness always embarrassed her.

In the first place he ought to have taken Mrs Jackson through to the cubbyhole office in the lobby at the back between the shop and the bakehouse, instead of keeping her standing there as he clomped about in his too-big boots serving customers with steaming bread and rolls, every now and again shooting a high-pitched whine of a question at her from a pink button mouth perched on top of a wispy goatee beard. The customers, crowding the shop, gossiped among themselves, stopping only to listen with unashamed interest to what was going on.

The last cleaner had moved to another district with her family, leaving one of the attic houses on the top flat empty. Now the spiral staircase of the three-flatted tenement above the shop that old Mr MacNair owned and let out to his employees was getting messier and messier. So was the shop itself.

The stairs and the bakehouse needed continuous scrubbing because of the rats, the cockroaches, and the flour puffing up in hot grey clouds that dried the nostrils and parched the throat. The flour, not content with continuously swirling in the air, solidified into a slippery paste underfoot to make the bakehouse, the lobby, the shop, the close, the stairs and the landings a dangerous ice-rink.

The cleaner's removal had put the old master baker out of temper, especially since one of her sons had worked in the bakehouse and her daughter had served in the shop.

Catriona had been deployed from her flat above to help in the shop until the new counter assistant arrived.

"No longer than one week," her husband Melvin had warned his father. "I don't want her wasting time gossiping to half the folk in Clydend. How's she going to have my dinner ready?"

Mrs Jackson was a widow and had been living alone in her house over in Townhead since her son Alec had married and moved to Springburn. Catriona had had the whole history before Mr MacNair had bothered to look at Mrs Jackson. The woman had rushed into conversation, a nerve twitching her eye like a wink. All about her son—what a good boy he was and how badly she missed him.

"His wife's a bit happy-go-lucky and extravagant. It worries me. Alec never complains but I know he worries too. It's the weans, you see." She leaned closer to Catriona as if concentration on her stare and its nearness would help Catriona to understand. "I'd like to help but I've only my widow's pension and what I get for a few hours' work in town. If only I could get this job at least I'd save on the rent."

Old MacNair collected rent from all those employees who occupied his flats, as had the last cleaner, but this time he had made up his mind to pay no wages and instead allow the new cleaner the attic flat rent free.

"You'll do!" his nasal whine announced at last. "Start on Monday and think yourself damned lucky."

"Cheeky bugger!" One of the customers turned to Mrs Jackson. "Don't pay any attention to him, hen."

A bright red collar of fire suddenly appeared round Mrs Jackson's neck and quickly burned her face to the roots of the dry-frizz of her hair.

"Thanks, Mr MacNair. Thanks."

The old man drowned her words by thumping a gnarled fist on the counter.

13

"Come on, come on! Who's next?"

Mrs Jackson squeezed between the customers to come back across to Catriona.

"Thank goodness that's over! Thank goodness!"

Catriona looked down with embarrassment.

"I'm glad you got the job." Holding her hair back with one hand, she stole an anxious glance at the older woman. "I hope you'll like it here."

She was secretly wondering if Mrs Jackson knew about the murder. The MacNair building in Clydend at the corner of Dessie Street and the Main Road had made headline news not so very long before. The Street of Tragedy all the papers had called it.

Sarah Fowler, wife of Baldy the foreman baker, had stabbed her mother-in-law in one of the flats upstairs. Never as long as she lived would Catriona forget the day when Sarah had appeared at the door, face apologetic, eyes bewildered.

I've kill't Baldy's mammy!

They had hanged Sarah in Duke Street prison and normal life as they had known it in the close at Number One Dessie Street had disappeared down the trap with her.

There had been other deaths, other changes. People had moved away, people had come to stare at the building.

Catriona herself had nearly died with a miscarriage.

"The trouble with you is you're too soft," her husband Melvin kept telling her. "You don't do enough physical jerks."

"Physical jerks!" Her mother saw red every time Melvin mentioned the words. "You wicked man. May God in His infinite mercy forgive you. You and your physical jerks were nearly the death of that girl."

Her mother had never forgiven her for marrying Melvin.

"Why? Why?" Even yet she kept asking, and she was always putting up prayers for her at the meetings of the Band of Jesus of which she was Grand Matron. "Why, Catriona? That man's old enough to be your father. He's been married before and has a child. You were only a child yourself. You weren't seventeen when you married that man. And what you saw in him I'll never know. A vulgar immodest ignorant man like that, and you such a well-protected, well-sheltered girl. I even insisted on being over in Farmbank instead of in Dessie Street so that you would have the benefit of being brought up in a respectable district."

She never tired of ranting on and on, digging mercilessly over and over again at old ground.

"It's your daddy's fault, of course. I've said it before and I'll say it again. If your daddy hadn't been off work with his filthy dermatitis that man would never have needed to come to the house to give your daddy his wages. And if he hadn't come to the house he would never have seen you and all this trouble would never have started."

Why had she married Melvin? She had repeated that "why" to herself far more often than her mother did. She had longed to leave her parents' house and have a place of her own. Perhaps that was the answer; yet Melvin's house had never felt and still did not feel a home of her own. It did not have the stamp of his dead first wife either, despite her photographs all over the house and the likeness in her little son, Fergus. It was Melvin's house. Everything belonged to him as he kept telling Catriona.

"Nothing's yours. You hadn't even a spare pair of knickers when you came here. By God, you were lucky when you got me, and don't you forget it."

Think yourself lucky. Think yourself damned lucky. How many times had she heard those words? *Be grateful.* She was grateful for having escaped from her mother but living with Melvin had given rise to the hypnotic fascination and the morbid fear of sleeping under the same roof as a dangerous animal. Often she dreamed of a friend to help and protect her and wistfully, yet without any real hope, she watched Mrs Jackson's golliwog head leave the shop.

"Here, you!" her father-in-law yelped. "Don't just stand there looking gormless. Get on with your work!"

Like a trapped bird beating its wings against the bars of its cage, Catriona flurried into action. Her hands delved into sacks to shovel up sugar and peas and beans and lentils and potatoes, her arm jerked backwards and forwards cutting sausages and black puddings, her fingers tinged over the till. Movement quickened her mind sending it racing ahead to wrestle with all the work waiting to be done in the house upstairs.

She became conscious of the metallic stammer of the riveters in the Benlin Yards across the Main Road. The racket was always there as if the whole of Glasgow was filled to the skies with blacksmiths. Often she managed to ignore it, to accept it as part of the savage background that life had acquired since her marriage to Melvin. But now it filled her head, drowning out the buzz of customers' voices and the jangle of the shop-door and the rattle and clash of trays and tins in the bakehouse at the back, and the kettle-drum tattoo of metal-rimmed cart wheels on the cobbled street outside.

Until suddenly even the Benlin riveters were banished by the shock of seeing her mother, straight-backed, big-chested and angry, in the shop.

"What is the meaning of this?" Ruddy, purple-veined cheeks mottled with anger she swung round to face Mr MacNair. "Are you trying to kill this child? Isn't one murder enough round here?"

"Mummy!" Catriona hissed, keeping her head well down in order to avoid everyone's eyes.

Her mother turned on her again.

"Get out from behind that counter and come upstairs at once!"

"But, Mummy!"

"Do as you're told!"

"Away you go, child," old MacNair's voice sniggered. "Do as your *mummy* tells you."

Trembling with humiliation Catriona came round beside her mother who immediately punched and pummelled her out of the shop, leaving behind whoops of laughter.

"I'm not a child."

"Oh, be quiet."

Mrs Munro shoved her into the floury close, sickly with the beery smell of yeast, and up the spiral stairs to the first landing.

"I'm not a child," Catriona repeated, but her trembling and the tears filming over her vision denied the words any authority. Her mother thumped on the door.

"I don't know what I have ever done to deserve all this worry. After all I've done for you, Catriona, after all the sacrifices I've made—and God knows I've made plenty, and I'm not taking the Lord's name in vain. After all these years . . ."

The door opened before she could say any more and Melvin, wearing striped pyjamas, the top lying open to reveal a hairy chest, stood glowering at her.

Catriona spoke breathlessly.

"I'm sorry, Melvin, Mummy knocked before I'd time to tell her I had the key."

Melvin flicked his eyes upwards in disgust and stomped away, his bare feet slapping loudly on the linoleum.

He was not a tall man, but Catriona was a fragile wisp of thistledown beside him. Melvin had an ape-like physique with a massive upper-arm measurement greater than Catriona's waist. Intensely proud of his muscle control he exercised religiously every day, giving a cringing Catriona a nude display of muscles bunching, twitching, hunching, circling.

"For a man working nights in a bakehouse, especially a man of my age, I'm a marvellous specimen," he never tired of telling her, despite his grey-white baker's face and the thinning hair that looked as if it had been parched with a lifetime's flour dust.

17

Now, not quite awake, he yawned and scratched his moustache as he returned to the bedroom, shouting out without looking round.

"I'm going to do my exercises. Put the kettle on."

"Listen to that!" Mrs Munro marched into the kitchen and jerked out the hatpin securing the hat on top of her thick coil of hair. "Lord Muck. He'll be the death of you yet, that man. You'll be the second he'll put under the clay, you mark my words."

Catriona lifted the kettle.

"Do you want a cup of tea?"

"I'll do it." Her mother snatched the kettle from her. "You go and sit down."

"I'm all right, Mummy. I wish you wouldn't worry."

"If you weren't so wickedly selfish I wouldn't need to worry. You have been punished, Catriona, and you will be punished again. He's watching you, Catriona. God misses nothing. Everything, every unkind selfish thought, every cruel disobedient act He takes note of and adds up for the terrible Day of Judgement when you'll stand before Him to await your final punishment."

She splashed water into the kettle, and clattered it on to the cooker. The gas lit with a plop.

"But make no mistake about this, Catriona, you'll be punished here too. For every sin you're guilty of, there's a punishment. Your disobedience, your ungratefulness, your wicked selfishness will be punished."

The words were so familiar to Catriona, her mind was mimicking the speech all the time a split second before her mother got there.

Yet despite the familiarity of the words and her bitter if silent attempts to discredit them, they had long since become part of her. It did not matter how much her mind struggled to reason in her own defence. It did not matter how much hatred and bitterness she conjured up to help her hit back. In her secret innermost places, the darkest corners of her mind, she was convinced of guilt, of unworthiness, and of the awful punishment and retribution that forever hung over her head.

Her eyes shrank down.

"I'm sorry . . . "

"There's no use . . . "

"Mummy."

" . . . being sorry. Do you want to die?"

"No, of course not."

"Well, why do you not have more respect for yourself? Stand up to the MacNairs, don't allow them to make a slave of you."

She strode about the kitchen finding cups and saucers, straight-backed, handsome, the sun from the window seeking out the burgundy richness in her hair.

"May God forgive the wicked villain! Fancy having you working down there in that shop after you've been so ill."

"There's a girl starting tomorrow."

"It's about tomorrow I've come. That man's dragging you off to the Exhibition, isn't he?"

"Yes, but . . . "

"I knew it!"

"But, Mummy."

"And you've agreed?"

"Everybody will be there. There's going to be people from all over the world."

"None of them will nurse you or care one jot when you're lying at death's door again. There's not a pick of flesh on you and he's going to make you crush through thousands of folk and walk for miles round and round, up hill and down dale in Bellahouston Park."

"I'll take a cup of tea through to Melvin."

"You'll do nothing of the kind. Put your feet up on that stool and drink your own."

"But Melvin asked . . . "

"If he wants tea let him come and get it. He's a lot more able than you. Let *him* go to the Exhibition!"

"Melvin wouldn't go without me."

"Let him stay at home, then."

"But I want to go to the Exhibition."

The door creaked open and Melvin, dressed only in loose-waisted trousers, came slowly into the room, concentrating on his exercises, his back, shoulder and upper arm muscles ballooning up.

"Where's my tea? See that tricep? There isn't another man in Clydend, probably the whole of Glasgow, with triceps like that."

"You ought to be black-burning ashamed!"

Mrs Munro averted her face, her ruddy cheeks darkening to purple.

"Ashamed?" Melvin's eyes bulged with incredulity. "What are you blethering about, woman?"

"Parading about half-naked. Displaying yourself."

"Good God, anybody would think I was walking up the middle of Sauchiehall Street."

"And don't blaspheme in front of me, either."

"Where's my tea?"

Hastily Catriona poured him a cup.

"Here you are, Melvin."

"Ta. My mouth feels like a sewer."

Mrs Munro's nose twisted and her eyes shrunk away again.

"You're disgusting!"

Melvin downed the tea as if it were whisky and wiped his moustache with the back of his hand before turning away to continue his exercises.

"Just you wait a minute," his mother-in-law commanded. "I've something to say to you."

"Eh?"

His attention was not really with her.

"You are not to take that poor child to the Exhibition tomorrow. She's not fit for it."

"Aw, shut up!"

He went away with his shoulders contorted into a grotesque hump that almost hid the back of his head. In a moment or two they could hear him cheerily whistling.

Chapter Three

From early morning, a rustle of excitement gathered momentum in the air. Purposeful crowds surged through the streets and squeezed together on buses, and tram-cars and trains rocking and rollicking them as they sped towards Ibrox and Bellahouston.

Limousines purred along fat with distinguished passengers. Family cars honked and rattled, windows busy with expectant faces.

The sun grinned down at Glasgow competing for attention with an exuberant gusty wind.

Soldiers lined the packed pavements of Union Street to keep the boisterous crowds in check as King George VI and his Queen made the twenty-five-minute journey from Central Station to Ibrox in an open landau drawn by four of the famous Windsor Greys, with outriders and postilions.

All along the route, tenement buildings leapt to life with whirling, lurching, rippling flags. Open windows were crammed with spectators fluttering handkerchiefs.

Inside Ibrox Stadium sixty-thousand people jamming together in good-humoured breathlessness. Great masses of children energising the crowd, Scouts, Cubs, Boys' Brigade, white-bloused Girl Guides like banks of daisies. The whole arena animating suspense, rocketing every now and again into cheers of relief.

The children screaming at everybody and everything. The stand filling with notables, lawyers, bright stars from the Scottish Offices in their silk hats; Lord Elgin's party and the little girl who was to present the bouquet to the Queen;

James Bridie, Will Fyffe, Sir Harry Lauder, all receiving resounding yells of welcome.

A groom busying himself about the lawn, paddock and pitch raising ear-splitting cheers. A policeman at the east end of the stand engaging in a nice bit of vaulting, falling on his face, and near-by Cubs roaring their hearts out.

Then twelve trumpeters appeared, scarlet and gold on the skyline like a row of toy soldiers, their fanfare blowing away in the wind and drowned by the great shout that welcomed the King and Queen as the Windsor Greys swept into sight.

Compared with the children the hearty cheering of the grown-ups was a performance without shape—self-conscious, ill-timed, hedged with Scottish shyness.

Alec let out a slightly derisive hurrah, then laughed and glanced round at his family to see if they too were laughing. He had the girls up on his shoulders and Madge had Maisie struggling in one arm trying to pull herself up by Madge's hair and Hector stamping and jumping about on her hip in his efforts to see over the heads of the crowd.

"My God!" Hilarity escaped from Madge in jerks and spasms. "I'm being murdered here."

"Ma's meeting us at Bellahouston. She'll take them off our hands."

"At Bellahouston? You're a scream! How are we going to find your ma at Bellahouston?"

"We'd better find her. We want to enjoy ourselves and not be lumbered with this lot."

Alec heaved his shoulders up and down, making Sadie and Agnes squeal with delight. And the squeals mingled with the cheers like a great fan, vivid with gaiety, pageantry and colour. The ceremony became a confused flicker of impressions distorted by excitement.

The King's voice fighting determinedly to defeat its stutter:

"Scotland believes that the best means of avoiding trouble is to provide against it, and that new enterprise is the safest insurance against the return of depression. It is in this spirit that the Exhibition has been built, and I see in it the symbol of the vitality and initiative upon which the continued prosperity of Scotland must rest."

The strong confident voices of the people joining together to deliver with gusto the Twenty-fourth Psalm: "Ye gates, lift up your heads on high . . . "

The machine-like smartness of the services led by the Navy and dressed by the right.

The fly-past seen from the start as sweeps of shadows at intervals across the grass.

Then the hurrying, pushing and heaving towards Bellahouston Park and the great Empire Exhibition of 1938.

Only one thing marred Tuesday the third of May for Sammy Hunter, and that was his promise to go to Balornock in the evening, when he and Ruth had been invited to have supper with his father, his stepmother and five of his eight brothers who had come up from England especially to be at the opening of the Exhibition. Then later in the week there was to be a return visit.

All his brothers had scuttled off to various parts of England as soon as they were old enough, getting as far away as possible from Balornock. Normally they only returned once a year, for Hogmanay, but the Exhibition was something that could not be missed.

The sixteen turnstiles at the Mosspark entrance clicked merrily, but as Sammy and Ruth crushed along in the queue, the thought of the two evenings with his father hovered over the back of his mind, black shadows threatening to engulf and reduce to insignificance the wonderful achievement of the Exhibition opening up in front of his eyes.

"We should have come earlier."

Head tipped forward as he walked he flashed a glance round at Ruth from under his brows, but Ruth's starry-eyed attention refused to waver from the impressive entrance with its sweeping curve, its slender pillars, its high fluttering flags.

"If your father's coming to us on Saturday we haven't much time to get the house all ready," she told him absently. "We'll have to do the shopping on Saturday afternoon."

Shadows lengthened and leaned forward. Yet he wanted his father and mother and brothers to come over on Saturday to see his new home. He was proud of his house, proud of the work that he and Ruth had done to it. They had transformed it from a rotting brown hovel, with rusted grate and flaking ceiling and wallpaper hanging from the walls, to a modern tastefully decorated home.

Ruth, of course, was his greatest pride and joy. A great cook and housekeeper, a wonderful lover and wife, she had the same passionate enthusiasm for setting a table, whipping up an omelette or bewitching him to the shuddering point of ecstasy in bed.

Often he wondered what she saw in him and then the miracle of their relationship seemed like a fragile bubble liable at any moment to burst in his guts and leave nothing but himself.

"Don't remind me of my father. Why do you always have to bring him up?" he grumbled.

"He's here, isn't he?" She shrugged. "We could bump into him, couldn't we?"

"In all this crowd there shouldn't be much chance of that."

"Who cares?" Ruth clutched his arm and squeezed it tightly against her breast. "Isn't this wonderful?"

They were inside now, staring at the Exhibition's greatest promenade and beyond it and above it in the distance the tree-encircled Bellahouston Hill with Tait's Tower on top— a giant of steel and glass that dominated the gleaming white city of palaces and pavilions below and the scores of smaller buildings spread gaily over the park from the foot of the hill, poetry in pastel shades of blue, red, yellow and french grey.

Who cared? He cared!

This was to be a day of days, a time of pride for Glasgow and the whole of Scotland. He wanted to bask in the glory and pleasure of it like everybody else. Nothing should be allowed to spoil it, especially for Ruth. Determination put length and purpose into his step, and Ruth began to giggle as she clipped along beside him.

They began pointing things out to one another, the lofty flagstaffs, the lake with its submarine floodlights and batteries of milky fountains, the pavilions competing with one another in splendour.

By the time they had worked their way round to the British Pavilion, even Ruth's effervescent spirits were beginning to go flat.

"Sammy, it looks wonderful but couldn't we save it for another day? We could come some Saturday afternoon, couldn't we, love? Or any evening after this week."

He squeezed her hand in acquiescence although he was keenly disappointed. He had been especially looking forward to seeing around the United Kingdom Government Pavilion with the great gilded lions at the doors of its entrance hall. This pavilion was said to be one of the most impressive in the Exhibition.

A pool or moat with a bridge across it from the main exit ran the entire length of the building. Scientific research was the theme of the exhibits inside and he had read in the papers how really sensational it was. The entrance hall was ninety-five feet in height and the exit had a gigantic steel and glass globe representing the world floating in space.

"My feet are killing me."

Ruth hopped on one foot as she bent down to remove a flimsy high-heeled shoe, wiggle her toes and empty the shoe of grit and dust.

"We could take one of the auto-trucks," Sammy suggested.

The thought of him with his self-conscious downcast glower perched back to back with another passenger on one of the little open auto-buses for everyone to see made Ruth's eyes brighten with mischievous laughter.

"I think I'll survive. But only if we don't trail round another pavilion. Can we just make our way round to Paisley Road now, love?"

"Wear sturdier shoes next time," Sammy growled, but both of them knew he didn't mean it.

They both liked to look smart. Ruth always wore high-heeled shoes and Sammy changed his shirt and put on a fresh starched collar every day of his life. Ruth was very particular about his clothes and he about hers. They always went shopping for clothes together, although going into the ladies' departments of a shop even with Ruth hanging on his arm was always an agony to Sammy.

He sighed.

Dust was swirling up with the wind and the shuffling of a hundred and forty-five thousand feet, parching his throat, stinging his eyes, and dragging heavily at his spirits, but perhaps it was only the thought of the impending journey to Balornock that depressed him.

He tried to throw the mood off in a sudden bluster of bravado.

"Come on, then, step it out smartly or you won't get any supper. The rest of the horrible Hunters will have eaten it all."

"Sammy!"

Squealing in protest, stumbling, choking with laughter she clung to his arm and struggled to keep up with his rapid strides.

"Sammy, will you stop it? Do you want me to get angry with you?"

"I'll have no insubordination from you, woman! You'll go over my knee as soon as we get home. You'll get a good thrashing if you don't watch your tongue!"

He came to an abrupt halt outside one of the Scottish pavilions high on terraced walls, patterned after North Country dykes, and boasting a many-windowed tower, an

26

immense statue of St Andrew in the entrance hall and a huge aggressive-looking lion rampant emblazoned in scarlet on the outside wall.

This Scottish lion standing on its hind legs, chest puffed, tail cocked, tongue curled, forepaws bunched up like fists sparring for a fight, was the emblem of the Exhibition.

There was something about Sammy, as he stared up at it, shoulders back, red hair spiking in the wind, that resembled the Scottish symbol. He had an aggressiveness, a prickling —"I'm ready for any comers—try me if you dare!"—outer covering that completely hid the man underneath.

"Good old Scotland!"

"Oh, Sammy, we're not going in, are we?" Her eyes, her body and her voice softened towards him. "Honestly, love, I'm exhausted. I'm not nearly as strong as you, don't forget."

He turned away. "Oh, there'll be plenty more chances before October."

The lofty Paisley Road entrance was in sight now but he stopped again, telling Ruth and himself that they could not leave without spending some time admiring the cascades, yet knowing that he was only succumbing to delaying tactics.

He stared solidly at the two giant staircases and the multi-coloured cascades leaping down from the top of the hill between them.

"Imagine that at night. Imagine this whole place floodlit."

"It looks marvellous right now. Everything does. I've never seen any place so marvellous."

"It's a grand achievement, this Exhibition. It shows what Scotland can do."

A pause grew in significance between them. Until at long last he broke the silence.

"All right. All right. Come on. We mustn't keep his bloody Majesty waiting!"

27

Chapter Four

"It's only fair that I should go home with Ma," Alec told Madge. "After all, Ma's the one who's been stuck with the weans all day."

Madge readily agreed.

"Aye, it's a damned shame." She tucked a lock of hair behind her ear and laughed. "Come on, hen."

"Not you, gorgeous. You go straight home and keep the kettle boiling for me."

Their cheerfulness grafted across the weary wailing of the children. Even Maisie, normally a gooing, dribbling cottage-loaf of good nature, was brokenhearted.

"These weans need their bed," Mrs Jackson accused her daughter-in-law. "It's terrible!"

Madge's freckled nose creased up.

"Och, right enough. Poor wee buggers!"

Alec gave her an encouraging pat on the shoulder, rubbed Maisie's baby head lolling helplessly against it and fondled the bottoms of his other three children, clinging round his wife's coat-tails.

"On you go with your mammy and you'll be all right."

"Da . . . dae!" Hector lamented and the twins took up the cry like a death-song.

Madge shifted Maisie on to her other hip so that she could give Hector a shaking.

"Shut up! Silly wee midden." Her tone was good-natured despite her words. There was always a hint of a cheerful guffaw behind everything Madge said. "You heard your daddy. He's to take Gran home. She's tired and fed up and I don't blame her."

"Those weans need their bed." Mrs Jackson spoke like a gramophone unable to get past one groove. "It's terrible!"

"Och, I know," Madge sympathised and struggled with her free hand to grab the clothes or whatever part she could of Agnes, Hector and Sadie. "And they've still to go all that way in the tram. I'd better get started."

"Right. See you later on, hen." With a quick convivial wave to his wife, Alec shepherded his mother off and both were soon carried away by the same crowd that was jostling Madge and the children, whose cries were fast reaching a crescendo.

"It's a disgrace," Mrs Jackson told Alec afterwards. "Fancy, poor tired wee bairns like that out on the streets when they should be in their beds. I always had you scrubbed spotless and asleep hours before this. These weans are always out till all hours. It's terrible."

"Aye, there's not many like you, Ma," Alec said, adding to himself, "Thank God," because half the time his mother talked a lot of nonsense. She had been out scrubbing here, there and everywhere and had never known when he was in bed and when he wasn't.

"Well, I'll leave you here, Ma." He put an arm round her shoulders and gave her a squeeze, when they'd left the tram-car and reached her close in Castle Street. "You'll be as right as rain now."

Her parchment skin tightened, bulging her eyes with panic.

"Aren't you coming up for a cup of tea, son?"

"Some other time, hen."

She leaned closer to him and gave him a conspiratorial nudge with a bony elbow.

"I might manage a wee nip of whisky in it. Just seeing it's you."

He spread out his palms and shrugged in a gesture of helplessness.

29

"It's the weans, hen. You heard them. They like me to be there."

She struggled to nod her agreement, almost an imperceptible movement at first as if her scraggy neck had locked.

"Aye." Her nod suddenly loosened, became briskly enthusiastic. "You're a good lad."

For no apparent reason a blotchy redness was creeping up from her neck to make her face look patchy.

"Cheerio then, Ma."

"Cheerio, son. When will I be seeing you again?"

The words hung uselessly in the air and he was away; spring-legged, shoulders swinging; his piercing whistle vying with the clash and clang of the tram-cars.

He was wondering what to do next when he literally bumped into Rita Gibson, a girl he used to work with, in more ways than one.

"Whoops!" He grinned down at her. "No need to rush me, gorgeous. Take it easy. I'm willing."

"Oh, it's you, Alec. Still the same as well. An arse for a mind."

"Aren't you lucky then, bumping into the only man in the world who's got two?"

"Aye, and my man'll kick you in both of them if he finds you with me."

'I'll bet five bob that right now your man's either at the Exhibition or in the pub."

She smirked an invitation up at him.

"Five bob? Is that all?"

He winked and jerked his head to indicate better things round the corner.

"Come on, hen!"

The house in Balornock was up near the park and Stobhill Hospital, a cottage facing Little Hill Golf Course in as near the country as one could get within the boundary of Glasgow.

It was a lonely place on a rough track that led to

Auchinairn and hidden from the Balornock Corporation housing scheme by the hospital buildings and the tree-thickened end of the park.

The nearest building to the cottage was the hospital morgue and many a nightmare the proximity of the place had given Sammy. He could vividly remember the terrors of coming home from school on dark winter nights, or returning from an errand and having to pass the place, a red brick coffin set well apart from the rest of the hospital. Worse still were the punishments imposed by his father. The "sentry duty", the "standing watch", the torment of being propped against the morgue and left there alone in the dark.

"Now, just ignore him," Sammy urged Ruth, automatically lowering his head and his voice as he approached the house. "Don't get upset."

Ruth made no reply as the garden gate squeaked open. They walked in silence through the shadows of the thick bower that made a low-roofed tunnel towards the door. Heavy trees crushed around the cottage blocking the windows and darkening the interior.

Sammy turned the handle and went in.

"Come on. Come on," he growled at Ruth. "There's no one waiting to jump on you with a gun."

But the mere sight of the place made anxiety descend on him like an invisible cloak of fleas.

They made their way in single file along the dark lobby and into the gloomy parlour.

Hodge Hunter stood huge and wide-legged, blocking the smouldering fire. Thumbs hooked in waistcoat, head sunk low in a coarse bull neck, he cocked a glittering eye at them.

"Well, well! Here's my youngest."

"How are you keeping, Mother?"

Sammy went straight over to his stepmother, a delicate little English lady, Hodge's third wife, and kissed her on the cheek.

"Oh, she's fine, fine." Hodge's sandpaper voice rubbed out Mrs Hunter's reply.

Sammy flashed a look of disgust before turning to his stepmother again.

"Ruth's going to help you with the tea."

"Well?" Hodge cut in hoarsely. "Where's my dram?" His voice surged up like sea roaring against rocks. "Stop simpering over your mammy. Give your old father a dram."

Hodge had made it a ritual on the few and far between occasions of family gatherings that everyone should toast the event and come well supplied with liquor for the purpose.

"Now, now, Father, don't be rude," Mrs Hunter chirped, smiling brightly round at Sammy's brothers, who could hardly be seen because the room was so shadowy and dark and they seemed to be shrinking back in their chairs as if desperately trying to make themselves invisible. "We ought to offer our guests a refreshment first. I have it all ready."

"You mean thon filthy slops you made the other day, you daft gowk! Do you want to poison us all?"

"Tt. Tt." Mrs Hunter clucked her tongue and flashed quick apologetic smiles all round. "He is a naughty man, isn't he? I've got whisky out as well, Father, but I thought perhaps Ruth might like to sample my raspberry."

"Prrr–rr——!" Hodge made a loud rude noise. "There's your raspberry!"

"For God's sake!" Sammy's face rivalled the dark red of his hair. "Stop behaving like an animal. You make me sick."

"I love your home-made wine," Ruth interrupted, coming forward with a defiant tilt to her head and a swing to her hips. "I can't stand whisky."

Hodge made a growling noise in his throat as if he were getting ready to spit.

"Ye've no taste in your mouth, woman."

Ignoring him, Ruth accepted the glass of wine Mrs Hunter poured out for her.

"Now, Sammy, here's yours, son. The boys have all got . . ."

"Here's to Scotland's grand Exhibition!" roared Hodge, swinging his glass high.

His sons eased cautiously to their feet to mumble down their whisky, but their father's voice, bawling out again, made them wince into silence.

"Here's tae us, wha's like us!" He flung back his drink, clattered the empty glass on to the mantelpiece, then screwed a fat neck round to his wife. "Where's my tea, woman?"

"I'm just away to the kitchen to dish it, Father. I've made a nice . . ."

"Come on, come on, jump to it." His sarcastic black beads of eyes straffed his sons. "Get round the table. Some have meat that cannot eat," he suddenly roared piously heavenwards. "Some no meat that want it. But we have meat and we can eat and so the Lord be thankit!"

"I'll come through and help you, Mrs Hunter," Ruth murmured, fluttering a worried glance at Sammy who was sitting down with the rest, eyes lowered like his brothers but fists white-knuckled.

"Well." Hodge marched stiff-legged over to take his chair at the head of the table. "I hope you come up with something better this time for your dinner was rotten!"

Sammy stood up and his stepmother immediately tinkled with laughter.

"Sh, Father, you rude silly man." Then brightly to Sammy, "Sit down, son."

Sammy was leaning forward, heavy-jowled and ugly.

"Don't worry," Mrs Hunter went on as if she were imparting exciting news to a crowd of favourite infants. "We're all going to have a lovely tea, and a lovely time, and everybody's going to enjoy themselves!"

33

Chapter Five

Catriona was terrified to tell either Melvin or her mother that she was pregnant. She dreaded the look of revulsion in her mother's eyes that would greet the announcement, the shrinking, the twist of the mouth and nose as if it was a filthy stinking disease Catriona was harbouring instead of a baby. She was caught in claustrophobia, unable to escape. The horror, the uncleanness, the guilt, was at the centre of herself.

Often she puzzled over her mother's attitude, at the same time not wanting to see the answer, dodging it, being temporarily reassured by her mother's insistent concern and dogmatic protestations of affection, yet all the time knowing what the answer was. Her mother hated her.

Only a few years ago, before her marriage, her mother's hatred of her had been made only too obvious. She had been panic-stricken by stabbing pains between her legs and a sudden gushing of blood that soaked her knickers and made her woollen stockings cling to her legs.

Shocked, and certain that she must have developed some dreadful disease, she hobbled through to the living-room where her mother was down on her knees raking out the fire.

"What'll I do? There's something wrong. I'm bleeding!"

"Get away from me!"

She could still see the turning of the head, the loathing in her mother's eyes, the screw of the nose and mouth against something foul smelling.

After that, not daring to mention the shameful bleeding

again, there had been many anguished months worrying about when she was going to die, months of secretly ferreting for odd bits of rags to mop up the blood, of trying to find efficient ways of securing the rags between her legs so that they would not fall out and shame her while she was at school.

She could not remember how or when she discovered that the bleeding was something known as menstruation and common to every woman—only that the knowledge had come too late.

The intimation of her first pregnancy had brought the same grimace, the same disgust to her mother's face. Only this time the words had been different.

"You poor child! A lot that man cares if you survive this ordeal or not. His first wife didn't!"

Melvin had puffed up with pleasure when he heard the news and immediately delivered a long lecture about animals and their similarity to humans, the tits of cows and the maternal instincts of female monkeys.

She had appealed to him to stop these uncalled-for and revolting comparisons but her distress had only encouraged him to launch into further explanations and illustrations.

Nature was a wonderful thing, he kept assuring her, hitching his shoulders and bulging his muscles to prove it. He insisted that she show him her abdomen and her breasts every day. He made her stand naked while he examined her and then, still naked, do exercises while he sat close, eyes bulging, a smile making his bushy moustache spread up.

He told her she must be massaged with olive oil or her skin would be ruined and when she protested he further horrified her by declaring.

"You'll have a belly like a plate of tripe. That's what happens when you don't get oiled. After the baby's born your belly will shrivel up like a plate of tripe."

So she had been oiled. Gleefully he massaged her while she stood in the middle of the room with head lowered trying to hide her growing deformity, her distortion, her unloveliness, by allowing her long fair hair to droop forward and her hands to act as tiny ineffectual screens.

Although Melvin and she were alone, she always felt her mother's eyes upon her, the stare growing and multiplying until every eye in the world despised her nakedness. The eyes never left her, could see beyond the outward sin to the greater sin inside, to the moment when despite self-loathing—she felt a quiver of pleasure.

The miscarriage had been her punishment, another scar in the mind, something to blank out and never speak of, yet a scar that would always be there.

The stabbing pain, the sudden gush of blood, the cry for help, this time to Melvin, and Melvin bawling out:

"For Christ's sake watch my good carpet! You'll ruin it. Wait till I get a pail or something."

Kneeling on the carpet unable to wait, the horror of the spreading stain, far outweighing her physical agony.

"I'm s-sorry, Melvin. I'm s-sorry, I'm s-sorry," she stuttered as he rushed about with pails and cloths before he even phoned for an ambulance.

Then the humiliations of the hospital examinations and the peculiar callousness of the abortion ward where doctors and nurses seemed to take it for granted that their patients, unmarried or married, had purposely caused their conditions. The whole staff were a vengeful God's representatives, whose duty it was to punish the miscarriers.

The thought of going through it all again appalled her. Even if she did not miscarry this time, the prospect was bleak. Her mother and her mother's friends had prepared her with plenty of gory tales about childbirth.

Most of all, she feared Melvin's reaction, and kept putting off the dreaded day of telling him until suddenly he said,

"For God's sake try and make a better job of it this time."

"A better job of it?" she echoed, eyes anxious to understand.

"You've got another bun in the oven, haven't you?"

"A bun in the . . . ?"

His eyes bulged upwards with impatience.

"Pregnant! Pregnant!!"

"Oh." She turned a deep pink, making the pale colour of her hair more noticeable in contrast. "Yes, I am." A delicate little sound as she cleared her throat. "And please don't start comparing me with animals, Melvin. I don't like it."

Melvin's moustache flurried out with a loud guffaw of laughter.

"I bet you don't like having a bun in the oven either but it's there, darlin'. You can't beat nature."

She tried not to tremble. She struggled to smooth calmness around her for protection because instinctively she knew that she must protect herself.

"It upsets me and I mustn't get upset while I'm pregnant."

"Well, don't!"

"There was nothing physically wrong with me before. They told me. It must have been caused by nerves."

"Well, don't have nerves. Physical jerks, that's the thing. And deep breathing." He widened his nostrils and expanded his chest to enormous proportions. "Nothing like physical jerks and deep breathing to keep you fit."

An aura of stubbornness descended on her. She lowered her head, this time not submissively, but aggressively.

"Don't talk about animals."

"'Don't talk about animals'," Melvin mimicked, then still with hilarity in his voice he added. "Don't you tell me what to talk about. I'll talk about what I like."

"Don't talk about animals and don't make me do exercises."

"Aw, shut up." He turned away.

"No, I won't. I won't."

The trembling was beyond control now—a series of rapid convulsions growing in strength.

"You're the one who's like an animal. No, you're worse. You're coarse. You're ignorant. You're insensitive. I wish I'd never set eyes on you. I wish I was home! I wish I was home!"

"With your holy cow of a mammy?" he sneered, swinging round on her, broad-shouldered and long-armed.

"I wish I was home!"

"What home, you idiot? 'Do not lay up for yourselves treasures on earth', your mammy's always quoting from her precious Bible, and she's carried it out to the letter, hasn't she? Your 'home' is as bare as a railway waiting-room and you hadn't a stitch to your back when you married me. Your mammy's that holy and generous she's given everything away. What have you got to go back to? 'Home', did you say?" He laughed again and suddenly pulled her into his arms. "Forget it!"

She could never credit how different marriage was from the fairy-tale land of women's magazines and romantic novels. She had read so many of them after she had left school only a few years ago, and they had been so cosy and enjoyable that no matter what happened, part of her would always believe them.

In fiction-fairyland the husband never knew about pregnancies until he was told and then, after being speechless with joy for a few minutes, he suddenly rushed for a chair to ease his wife into as if she were made of the most delicate, the most precious china.

After that, during the whole pregnancy in fact, he watched her anxiously while she kept laughing and assuring him that she was perfectly all right. And she *was* perfectly all right, except perhaps for little fads and fancies like wanting a melon or a bowl of soup in the middle of the night, when the husband would walk miles searching for titbits.

In real life she had once taken a terrible craving for chips. She was usually in bed alone most of the nights because Melvin worked downstairs in the bakehouse but

38

this had been his night off and she had timorously tugged at his arm until he had grunted awake.

"Whassa matter, eh?"

"Melvin, I'm sorry, but I fancy some chips."

"You must be joking, darlin'."

"No," she assured him. "I'd love some chips." Her mouth watered at the thought. "With plenty of salt and vinegar."

"Chips be damned!" he chortled, pulling her towards the hot sweaty smell of his body. "I know what you want!"

"No, Melvin, please!" She tried to flurry away his octopus hands but he jerked on top of her, his massive shoulders and hairy chest pinning her down gasping for breath.

Sometimes she hated the writers of romantic fiction for deceiving her so outrageously and yet all the time she longed for their rosy, gentle world and hoped that one day she might find it.

The only person in the family who took the news with acquiescence was Fergus, her stepson.

"You'll like having a little baby brother or sister, won't you, Fergie?" She knelt down in front of him and held his hands together.

"Yes, thank you," he replied, his blue eyes empty.

"Oh, you will, you will!" she repeated more to reassure herself than the child standing so still in his scuffed shoes and drooping socks and school-cap slightly askew.

Her mind was speeding along two concurrent lines. She would have to tidy Fergus up before Melvin saw him or she would get a row. Melvin was almost as fussy about the care of Fergus's clothes and person as he was about the scrubbing and polishing of everything in the house.

"My house", he often expostulated, "has always been the best furnished, best-looking place in Clydend and I want it kept that way. There isn't another floor in the whole of Glasgow that's ever had such a marvellous polish as that!"

Or about Fergus he would hitch back his shoulders and boast:

"That child is the best-behaved, best-mannered, most obedient child in Scotland."

Indeed, for most of the time with adults, and especially with his father, Fergus was a model of quiet perfection.

Yet he was capable of unexpected extremes of emotion that frightened Catriona.

Sometimes she would walk past him when he was playing contentedly on the floor, or so it seemed, and suddenly he would lunge at her, clinging to her legs and hugging them with the strength of a maniac who would never let go. More than once after unsuccessful attempts to free herself, she had panicked and screamed for Melvin. But when Melvin arrived on the scene Fergus was always innocently playing with his toys again as if nothing had happened.

Now, since he had started school odd reports were reaching her of violent behaviour towards other children.

"You'll love a little brother or sister, and look after it, and be kind to it, won't you?"

"Yes, thank you," Fergus replied.

She released his hands and allowed him to walk away. He was a strange child.

She struggled to her feet to stand absently nibbling at her nails. She felt far from happy.

Chapter Six

Sammy marched along Clyde Street from the office of the wholesale warehouse where he worked, hands in pockets, eyes down on shoes. Normally when he reached the Saltmarket he jumped on a tram-car for home. This time he decided to stretch his legs and walk for a bit.

The Balornock ordeal was well in the past, with time deadening it, pushing it further and further away like a comforting growth of cotton wool. The return visit had become another milestone that he tried to leave far behind him too. Although visions still streaked across his mind's eye, and every now and again an echo startled him.

He hated his father's voice. It made him feel sick. His father sounded as if he were perpetually gathering phlegm in his throat in readiness to spit. His voice had the unnerving habit of changing in tone and volume, for no apparent reason. Even a normal remark about the weather was liable to swell into a lion-sized roar. It see-sawed between correct, carefully intonated English and a coarse Scots dialect that twisted into a sneer.

Sammy hated the sound of his father's voice but even more he hated his silences.

He had watched him enter the house in silence and silently march around poking at things with his heavy silver-topped stick as if he were conducting a kit inspection. He watched until he could bear it no longer. Ruth and he were painfully proud of their room and kitchen, proud but unsure. They had in their eagerness for originality and perfection experimented with colours and new ideas, and spent rather more than they could afford.

"There's still a lot we'd like to do," he burst into his father's silence eventually. "But we've had to call a halt. It's a question of money."

Hodge poked underneath a cushion, caught a silk stocking on the end of his stick and hitched it high in the air.

"You've had to call a halt!" his voice exploded before settling down to a hoarse rasp. "About time, too!"

He had secretly cursed Ruth's untidiness, while knowing perfectly well that his father was to blame for purposely coming too early, before she had time to put everything away.

All the same he cursed her afterwards and a bitter quarrel had shattered the last remnants of pleasure in their grand new home. Until later, lying stiff and unhappy in the darkness beside her in the cabinet bed he felt her toes and her fingers begin to edge caressingly towards him. Then her body wriggled gently nearer, melting his misery with its warmth and its voluptuous quivering flesh. She began kissing every part of him except his mouth although his mouth sought hers with increasing anxiety.

His temples, his eyes, his ears, her tongue tickling and exciting in exploration. The hollow of his neck, deep under his arm, his belly, his groin.

His pace lengthened and quickened after turning left into the Saltmarket. He banished Ruth from his mind and concentrated instead on his immediate surroundings.

Many famous names had been associated with the Saltmarket. Oliver Cromwell had lodged in the street when he occupied Glasgow. King James VII had visited a house here when he was Duke of York. Daniel Defoe had walked along this street. But it had been a different place in those days. Some hundred-odd years after Defoe's visit, the Saltmarket and the near-by streets, Goosedubs, Bridgegate, King Street, Trongate, High Street and Gallowgate had been described as "a citadel of vice". Within less than one sixteenth of a square mile there were a hundred and fifty shebeens and two hundred brothels.

Glasgow had been and still was a grim city. Yet it had a bouncy pulse of humanity and a humorous quirk that was the very essence of the place.

He liked the story about the crowds outside the Justiciary buildings in Jail Square on the left side of Saltmarket. Glasgow folk love a pageant, a procession, any kind of show, and crowds always gathered to watch the beginning of each High Court, with the trumpeters and the solemn-bewigged judges. A crowd gathered at the end of each big trial across the road at the entrance to Glasgow Green. The police, fearing trouble from the supporters of gangsters who had just been sentenced, and danger to witnesses leaving the court-house, decided it was imperative that something should be done. There was only one way to disperse a mob at this particular spot. The Parks Department of Glasgow Corporation planted a few flower-beds to break up the open space. No Glaswegian, not even a gangster, would trample over a flower-bed. Even a gangster being chased by a policeman would make a detour round a flower-bed and the policeman chasing him would do the same.

The South Prison used to be in Jail Square and prisoners were hanged in public outside it. The last thing a condemned person saw before he died was Nelson's monument in Glasgow Green—a fact which gave rise to the Glasgow insult, "You'll die facing the Monument".

The last person hanged there was an Englishman, a Doctor Pritchard who had poisoned his wife and mother-in-law in his house in Sauchiehall Street. Thirty thousand men, women and children had gathered to watch the hanging in eighteen sixty-five. Bakers and piemen did a roaring trade and as usual on these occasions, including the years when pickpocketing was a hanging offence—pickpockets did their best business.

Sammy saw a white tram coming and raced for it.

43

A memory of his father had caught at his guts and the sudden burst of energy helped to excoriate it.

His father would have enjoyed public hangings. To watch someone suffer puffed him up with glee and to deliver the punishment himself was a luxury he indulged in as often as possible.

The Hunter family had always been organised along military lines. They mustered to attention by the sides of their beds at the crack of dawn for kit inspection. Then they route-marched to the park every morning before school and twice on Sundays and round and round inside the park before having to perform violent exercises to the sergeant-major roar of their father.

Some of the older brothers had been lucky. They could remember a spell in their youngest days when Hodge had been away from home. Sammy being the last born had had no such luck.

Punishments ran along military lines, too—square bashing, at the double, and in full kit, and full kit could be anything heavy his father managed to find with which to weigh them down. Detention was being locked all night in the coal-cellar. Duty watch meant the mortuary. Hodge had also delved back in time and come up with punishments the army had long since abolished, like flogging and the old army custom of branding.

Only once had the latter punishment been meted out and Sammy had been the recipient.

His father had been asking the family, one by one, what regiment they would join if ever their country needed them. Each brother in turn mumbled the regiment of his choice but when it came to his turn, hatred suddenly rocketed up to distort his features and rush bile to his mouth with the word:

"None!"

"What regiment?" His father's face blocked sight, filled the whole world.

"None!"

44

"What regiment?"

"None!"

He could see the first wave of shock receding and the vision of punishment to come taking its place.

"Eh? Eh? . . . What's this? What's this? Would you not fight for your King and country?"

"No."

"You're a disgrace to the name of Hunter. You're a bloody coward!"

His own mother had been alive then, a pathetic shadow of a women, and he always believed the ceremonial sadism of his branding had been the last straw that had killed her. His stepmother, not having been dragged down by constant child-bearing and the burden of his father, and having perhaps a spunkier nature, might have gone to the police for help, where his own mother struggled to protect him and failed.

The deep scar on his chest was still there.

He had told no one the truth of its origin, not even Ruth, brushing aside questions with irritable hints of road accident injuries.

He stared with grey marble eyes out of the tram-car window. It had left the Saltmarket, trundled beyond it up High Street, rocked round the bulge that was Castle Street before the long stretch of road from the Saltmarket straightened out again and became Springburn Road.

He allowed his body to rock and jerk with the motion of the tram and his mind open to the whirling grind of it as it struggled up the steep gradient towards the heart of Springburn.

First stop in Springburn Road—St Rollox works. Three stops past that—Springburn Cross. There at the hub of Springburn two streets diverged from the main road, Cowlairs Road on the left leading to Cowlairs Locomotive Works and Vulcan Street to the right leading to the main gate of Hyde Park Locomotive Works.

Over the railway bridge now at Springburn Station and

the Atlas Works. Where else in all the world, it occurred to him, his spirits surfing on a wave of pride, could a passenger in a tram-car, in the course of a half-mile journey along a public highway, have found such a concentration of railway skills. Company works, private builders, major sheds, and a mainline cable-worked incline.

Away to the west, cranes of the Clyde shipyards spiked the sky. To the north stretched the magnificent sweep of open country across the Kelvin Valley to the Campsie Fells and the first West Highland mountains, including Ben Lomond and Ben More.

But down here where he lived was the next busiest part of Springburn to the Cross. The tenement houses, all with shops below, were old and often dilapidated but there was a homely buzz of life around them. Springburn was a beehive, always busy, busy with people, busy with movement, busy with talk. Traffic passed ceaselessly to and fro, courting couples swung along hand in hand, mothers heaved energetically at prams, and there were always railwaymen in dungarees and shiny caps going on their shifts or coming off with black, soot-smeared faces.

He warmed to the place as he crossed the road to the corner where the usual crowd of men were standing arguing about football. Children were thumping a ball in his close and singing in light bouncy voices:

"One, two, three, a leary. Four, five, six, a leary, seven, eight, nine, a leary, ten a leary postman!"

He ran up the stairs his young-old face brightening to find Ruth with the door open and arms wide waiting for him. He grabbed her waist and made her squeal with excitement as he heaved her up and whirled her round and round their freshly painted hall.

Then suddenly he stopped. He held her close, one hand pressing her dark head hard against his shoulder.

He shut his eyes. He prayed for the sadness to go away—and with it the premonition of something terrible, not in the nightmare past, but something still to come in the future.

Chapter Seven

"Get your hands off my man!"

Madge battered through the swing doors of the insurance office just as Jean, one of the typists, was struggling with breathless laughter to forcibly remove Alec from her chair.

Draped nonchalantly back, his long legs propped on top of her typewriter, Alec had been enjoying the girl's hands tugging at him and her breasts bulging over the top of her blouse as she jerked back and forward under his nose.

The sudden arrival of his wife knocked both the typist and himself off balance.

"You rotten selfish little tart."

Madge advanced, big-boned, high-hipped, feet and hands like spades.

"Playing around with a married man—and him with four weans!"

"No! No!" Jean protested. "You've got it all wrong."

"Oh, come on, gorgeous!" Alec slid between them and pinched Madge's pale freckled cheek. "As if anybody could lure me away from you."

Madge knocked him aside.

"I was told about you," she loudly accused the typist again.

"About me?"

"You heard."

"What about me?"

"You've been seen going around with my man, hanging on to him like a leech. I'll leech you!"

"Alec!" the girl appealed.

"I'll Alec you!"

Madge's hand shot out and found bull's-eye on the girl's nose. Blood spurted in the silence for a horrified moment before Jean managed to wring out a long agonised scream.

Alec tugged at his wife's arm.

"Madge, for pity's sake, come on home before they get the police to us."

The normally quiet sedate routine of the office had switched to uproar and typists were running, whinnying for Mr Torrance.

"Quick!" Alec urged, putting his arm round Madge and hauling her off. "Before old Torrance arrives!"

As he told her later, on the angry march home:

"You'll be lucky if I'm not ruined and you're not in the nick by tomorrow. Then what would the weans do?"

"Women like that ought to be shot." Madge tucked a straggle of short hair behind her ears then suddenly grinned. "I did not bad, though, considering I hadn't a gun."

They plunged into the gloom of the pend, their feet echoing like a stampede of wild horses.

"But look, Madge, I've enough trouble tangling with women at work without you making things worse."

"I was there to help you." Her voice became angry again. "You ought to see Mr Torrance. You ought to tell him, Alec."

"Tell him what?"

"That women won't leave you in peace."

"What can he do, hen? Except tell me to pack in the job. The married ones are the worst," he confided. "Some of the houses I go to—my God, I've to fight them off."

"Which houses?" Madge stopped at the foot of the outside stairs, one red hand gripping the railing. "Tell me which ones. I'll fight them off all right."

"Sparrin' for a barney, eh?" One of their neighbours, leaning on her window sill, plump arms folded to support her big chest, cosily joined in the conversation.

48

"It's a bloody wee midden in the office trying to get away with my man."

"No!" Mrs White looked suitably shocked.

Alec shook his head.

"Honest to God, hen," he appealed to the neighbour. "It beats me where she got the idea."

"Mary down the road told me 'A girl you worked with' she said," Madge explained. "Saw her hanging on to you like a leech and hauling you up a close in Castle Street."

Gazing up at the older woman, her voice loudening, she added: "And when I went in to the office today to find out which wee midden it was—I caught her—carrying on before my very eyes!"

"No!"

Alec chortled out loud. A case of mistaken identity. "Mary down the road" must have got her beady eye on him on one of his visits to Rita Gibson.

"Madge gave her a straight right."

Alec began jerkily sparring, head down, fists jabbing backwards and forwards, as he bounced up and down on the balls of his feet.

"And then a left hook and then a quick one, two, three to finish her off!"

With a howl of hilarity Madge punched and unbalanced him against the stairs.

"I gave her a bloody nose though!"

"No!"

A smell of kippers and ham and eggs titillated their nostrils. Windows were open, frying pans sizzling, getting-ready-for-high-tea-happy-sounds.

A little girl jumped up and down, legs twisting and knotting as if desperate to hold in water.

"Mammy, Mammy!"

"What is it?" (A bawl from inside one of the houses.)

"Mammy, fling me a jeely piece."

"Yer tea's nearly ready."

"Och, I'm starving."

Then like manna from heaven a piece of bread, spread liberally with jam, sailed out one of the top windows.

"Come on." Alec made a rush at the stairs. "I'm starving as well."

The children had been left in the house while Madge went round to the office and they spilled out with the dog the moment she opened the door. In a few months' time there might be another to add to the rush because Madge had "missed" again. He hoped she was pregnant. Nothing like a baby to keep a woman out of mischief.

"Right, hen!" His hand slid between her buttocks and underneath to tickle her as the children milled around them. "I'll go through to the room and have a look at the paper while you get the tea ready."

His finger kept twitching the back of her dress as he walked close behind her, until she smacked at his hand.

"Get off!"

He went through to the room whistling and glad that his brood had followed their mother into the kitchen in the hope of something to eat.

The sight of the old roll-top desk reminded him of work and his mouth twitched. A case of mistaken identity—poor old Madge, always blundering into something or other. Just in case she blundered into Rita Gibson he had better be careful.

He had been making a habit of Rita since bumping into her the day the Exhibition opened. Her man was an engine-driver at Eastfield and worked shifts. Railwaymen worked damnable hours—never the same ones from one week to the next. His shifts went all round the clock, starting at a different time each week. He was older than Rita—past it probably—that would explain her insatiable appetite. Just could not get enough. He would have to cut her down. She was a right hairy.

Now take Ruth Hunter. She was different—a plum; ripe, succulent, juicy.

The door opened, interrupting an imagined energetic grapple with Ruth.

"I've given the weans theirs," Madge announced, slapping her bottom down on a chair. "So that we can have ours in peace after." She slumped back. "God, Alec, I'm tired!"

Now that he looked at her, he could see she was pregnant. Thick-waisted and high-bellied she sat with her knees splayed out and her hands hanging helplessly in the hollow of dress at her groin.

"Och, never mind, hen," he comforted. "I'll stay in tonight."

Her freckled face brightened and she gave him a big grin.

"You mean it?"

" 'Course I do."

"There's a good programme on the wireless."

"Mm-mm!" He winked. "Nothing as good as the programme I've lined up for you!"

She laughed but her enthusiasm tailed off a little.

"No kidding, Alec. I'm beat."

He came across to hunker down in front of her and slip his hand gently up her skirt.

"You won't have to do a thing. You'll just lie back and relax and enjoy yourself."

"Get off!" she protested, but remained in the same slumped back position as if she had not enough energy to move.

She sighed.

"You're a randy bugger."

"Aren't you lucky!" he said.

"I'll kill you if you leave me for that wee midden in the office. And I'll kill her as well. Becky McKay's man went away and left her and she had to go to the poorhouse. Fancy! Becky McKay's in Barnhill and she gets chucked out every morning with all her weans. She's to walk the streets all day until they let her back in at night."

With a jerk she awakened from her reverie.

"Alec!"

A stampede along the lobby made Alec sit back on the floor and Madge tug her skirts down just in time, as the door burst open and Sadie and Hector came yelling into the room.

"He stole my piece," Sadie accused. "I was helping Maisie eat her tea and he stole my piece."

"Didn't! Didn't! Sneaky big clipe!"

Alec suddenly let out a bear growl and lunged at them on his hands and knees and they went hopping and skipping back along the lobby, with Alec after them, their fury changing to hysterical screams of excitement.

Madge followed, tucking her hair behind her ears and laughing.

The kitchen was small and hot because even in summer the fire had to be on to heat the oven at the side, and the hobs on top for cooking.

"It's sausages." She tried to make Alec hear above the din. "Do you want a couple of eggs with them?"

Alec got up and enjoyed a good stretch.

"I'll take anything you've got to offer me, gorgeous!"

"That's three slices of sausage and a couple of eggs."

She grinned, adding good-humouredly to Sadie, "Grab that bread knife from Maisie, hen, she's going to kill herself!"

Alec leaned over the iron sink to peer for a minute out the window into the yard below.

He felt good. Life was good.

Turning back to his family and his tea he began to sing.

"Pack up your troubles in your old kit bag and smile, smile, smile . . . . "

The children joined in, banging their spoons.

"What's the use of worrying? It never was worth while— so-o-o . . . . !"

Chapter Eight

Catriona's baby was due in November and now, seven, nearly eight months pregnant, it looked as if she was not going to miscarry. The baby heaved and kicked violently inside her. She could actually see it lumping up her smock as she sat resting her aching back against a pile of cushions on one of the sitting-room chairs.

It was obscene. She averted her gaze from herself but her eyes kept returning to stare at the jolting, mountainous abdomen.

"Is that the bell?"

Melvin flung down his newspaper as Catriona heaved herself up.

"I'll go."

"Sit still! I'll see who it is."

"I want to go." She glared at him. "I'm fed up sitting still."

He bulged his eyes heavenwards and reached for his newspaper again.

A tall good-looking man stood at the door. Despite her misery and the hundred and one aches and pains that plagued her, dragged her down with the ponderous weight, she experienced a tiny thrill. The slim body, the dark hair, the twinkling eyes, reminded her of young Jimmy Gordon, the confectioner in the bakehouse who had died so suddenly.

Her eyes shrank down, her cheeks crimsoned with the shame of her appearance. Shutting the door a little she whispered round it.

"Yes?"

Alec grinned and winked at her.

"Hello, you gorgeous doll. I'm Alec Jackson and I've lost my mammy."

Her hand flew to her mouth to stifle an unexpected giggle.

"I know I'm a big boy," he said. "But it's true."

"Isn't Mrs Jackson upstairs?"

"Everybody in this stair must be dodging me, hen. I've knocked on every door and you're the first wee soul that's answered."

"Maybe she's down in the shop."

"You're a genius!"

Another almost imperceptible giggle was captured in her hands and timorous eyes peeped expectantly up at him.

He puckered his lips and bunched his fingertips against them to flick a kiss towards the gradually narrowing crack in the door.

"And a gorgeous wee blondie as well!"

The door clicked shut and she shuffled flat-footed back across the hall, rocking from side to side, a tiny boat a-bob bob bobbing.

"Well?"

Melvin's mustachioed face rose from the top of his paper.

Catriona slumped into the cushions.

"Well, what?"

"What do you mean, 'Well, what'?" His eyes protruded with indignation. "Who was that at my door?"

"Somebody looking for Mrs Jackson." She shifted about irritably, restlessly. "Anyway, it's not your door!"

"Not my door? Jumpin' Jesus, you're going off your nut like your mother."

"If it's any kind of door, it's *our* door. Everything's always yours, yours, yours."

"Well, everything *is* mine!"

Her fists bunched on her lap as if keeping a tight grip on tears.

"Nothing belongs to me and I don't belong anywhere."

"What are you blethering about now?"

"Oh, shut up!"

"Don't you tell me to shut up!"

"Shut up! Shut up! Shut up!"

Melvin tossed his newspaper aside and stretched to his feet menacingly to hitch and bulge huge muscles over her.

"What are you going to do?" she queried, her personal discomforts niggling her far beyond fear. "Challenge me to a wrestling match?"

He held his pose for a shocked second, then suddenly he flung back his head in a loud bellow of laughter.

She could not help laughing herself, although the hilarity that made her shiver in her nest of cushions was dangerously near the opposite extreme of heartbroken tears.

Melvin perched his heavy bulk on the side of her chair and put a gorilla arm round her shoulders.

"That's not a bad idea! Give us a kiss!"

Dodging his lips she pecked at his cheek.

"Melvin, I'm sorry but I'm absolutely exhausted. I'm fit for nothing until I get a cup of tea. Would you like to make it, dear? You do it so much better than me."

She watched him hesitate and saw in his face the fear that he might be endangering his manhood. She pecked him again.

"I don't know what I'd do without your strength at a time like this. I feel absolutely useless!"

He guffawed with laughter.

"You are useless! Stay there. I'll go and make the tea. But you'd better enjoy it and be grateful, do you hear?"

"Yes, thank you, Melvin."

He went through to the kitchen and she closed her eyes and sat with her arms hanging limply over the arms of the chair. She tried to relax. She tried to think pleasant thoughts to help her relax. It was no use. Her eyes opened; annoyance, vexation, harassment, elbowing for expression. Every few second she had to move, to hitch herself clumsily from one position to another, working herself through a hundred minute variations of body and limbs. And still she could not find a comfortable position.

Then she took an unbearable pubic itch. She looked furtively around to make sure that neither Melvin nor anyone else could see her, before having an exquisite scratch.

She felt sore, sore in the groin, sore in the back, sore in the breasts—her tiny boyish breasts now swollen, brown-stained, blue-veined.

In sudden pique she jerked her head from side to side at the same time bouncing her shoulders up and down, like a spoiled child stamping in a tantrum made worse by being so cruelly weighed down.

Her flurry of revolt against the injustice of it all gave her a throbbing headache and brought weak tears of defeat.

The only consolation she could find was that in a few weeks it would all be over. No more restlessness, no more having to trot to the lavatory every fifteen minutes and less at night. Her need to pass water had become so frequent she was like a sleepwalker staggering in and out of bed, in and out of the bathroom, the whole night long.

No more not being able to keep her stockings up, or fasten her shoes, no more indigestion and heartburn, no more gluttonous cravings that made her sick with shame.

For days now, unknown to Melvin, she had been consuming, one after the other, half-a-dozen rhubarb tarts. Fergus had caught her the other night and had stood, mouth drooling, dying for just one. But she had childishly clutched the box in her arms and told him to go away.

Porridge was another thing! She had greedily supped potfuls and potfuls of the stuff, often horrifying both Melvin and Fergus by wolfing into a tin of fruit salad immediately afterwards.

She would not be a bit surprised if, once the birth was over, she could never face porridge or fruit salad. She was perfectly certain that she would never, never look at her bottle-green bell-tent of a swagger-coat again.

Never! Never! Never!

Tears gushed faster. How did she know she would ever be herself again. How did she know she would have the strength to survive the terrible unknown ordeal yet to come.

If only she could close her eyes and open them to find it had all been a nightmare. Hopefully, she tried it, though she knew there was no escape. The knowledge that she was trapped had been steadily closing in on her like unknown assailants in a pitch black room.

Terror that defied expression shuddered from her roots, clawed up years of black indoctrination, dogmatically instilled fear, ignorance, enforced severance from her contemporaries, imprisonment in her mother's iron womb.

"What's wrong now?" Melvin asked when he returned carrying a tray of tea-things.

A minute or two passed as her sobs racketed wilder and she was unable to speak.

Unnerved by the unexpectedness of the outburst Melvin put down the tray and in his haste slopped tea in to the saucers.

"Hell's bells!" he roared. "Now look what you've done!"

"M . . . M . . . Melvin!" she managed to choke out eventually. "I'm . . . I'm . . . frightened!"

"Frightened? Frightened of what?"

"M . . . M . . . Melvin! M . . . M . . . Melvin!"

He smacked a shovel of a hand against his brow.

"Jumpin' Jesus!"

"Please help me!"

He hesitated, his face screwed with an exasperation that quickly relaxed into a chuckle.

"Come here!" He stomped over and sat down in the chair opposite her. "Come over and sit on my knee."

57

She nodded, jerky and hiccoughing with sobs. Eagerly her hands clutched at the arms of her chair. She pulled, and heaved, grunted and wriggled, rocked and kicked out her legs but was unable to get up.

Melvin began to laugh. Tears of laughter dripped down and wet his moustache.

"Come on!"

She kept trying, breathless now, and skin shining with sweat, eyes big and soft and tragic like a seal's.

Until she stood in front of him, her strange heart rapidly pittering, and above it her own heart pounding with grief.

She knew at that moment whas it was really like to be a woman, and she would never forget it as long as she lived.

"Come on!" Melvin chortled, loudly smacking his knees. "Don't just stand there like an elephant!"

She waddled a few steps, pushing her abdomen in front of her and thankfully eased herself down on his lap. Then with a long shuddering sigh her head collapsed back against his shoulder.

"I know what you need," Melvin said, his hand already searching out her breast.

"No."

"I know what you need, better than you know yourself!"

"No!"

He pulled one tender milky breast from blouse and brassière, balanced it on his palm then flipped and smacked it up and down.

He was settled back in his chair, relaxed, taking his time, enjoying himself.

God who was a man, God who made all men, she thought, damn Him!

Chapter Nine

The Exhibition flag on the tower was to be lowered at midnight on Saturday, 29 October, to signify the end of the Empire Exhibition to which Glasgow had been generous host.

Enormous crowds flocked to Bellahouston Park to enjoy the sights and smells and sounds of the Exhibition before the gates were locked for the last time.

Alec, Madge, his mother and the children went for an hour or two in the afternoon. Alec took the children on a screaming hilarious trip through the amusements park, the giant wheel, the stratoship, the whirler, the crazy house with its walls and windows all out of perspective and its noisy mechanical cats. There they all wandered about eating new pink clouds of sugar called candy floss, and licking the latest thing from Canada—a whipped up whirl of ice-cream.

A special air of gay abandon stirred among the vast crowds, a determination to toss all Scottish caution to the winds and whoop it up, enjoy themselves before everything packed up and went away.

Alec was no exception. He planned to take Madge and the family home and come back on his own to really have a time of it. After all, poor old Madge could not be expected to whoop it up. She was more likely to drop it down.

Anyway she had developed varicose veins, and something had gone wrong with her ankles, in fact she seemed to be puffing up like a balloon all over. He had never seen her look such a mess. Her hair, mousy at the best of times, hung lifeless and greasy. One of the neighbours had cut it for her and made it too short at the back and too long at the sides. Patches of white skin showed at the nape of her neck but two lank tufts of hair kept straggling forward to cover her ears. Her freckles looked worse, too. Clusters of them seemed to have joined together to make brown smudgy patterns. The only decent things left about her were her eyes, wide-apart, bright candid blue, and that big-toothed grin she could always come up with.

"I think it's time I got you safely back home, hen." He squeezed an arm as far as he could round the swollen waist. "I don't want you collapsing here and being trampled underfoot by a mob like this."

His mother's mouth worked with emotion.

"He's a good lad."

"Aye," Madge agreed, wiping away the remains of her ice-cream with the back of a red work-roughened hand. "Alec is good to me, so he is!"

She had never been a daft sentimental type, but the love in her eyes as she smiled up at him was suddenly embarrassingly obvious.

He gave her bottom an affectionate pinch.

"Right, home to bed with you!"

"God! Home to bed, he says!" She flung back her head with a shout of laughter. "And him has to go out collecting and me all the weans to feed and put down."

"Now, now," Mrs Jackson reprimanded. "Count your blessings. You've got a good man, he's out day and night struggling to make enough to feed you."

"Och, I know," Madge agreed.

"I'd come and see to the weans only I'm supposed to clean that . . . that what you call it?"

"Bakehouse," Alec prompted.

Sometimes he thought she was going mad. In her bouts of forgetfulness his mother had been known to forget her own name.

"That's right. Clean that bakehouse before the late ones

come in and you should see the place. You should just see what I've to do. I've to take a knife to that floor. Imagine! A knife to scrape it! It takes me hours and it's just as bad again the day after."

"Och, it's a damn shame." Madge scratched her belly. "I'd be over giving you a hand if it wasn't for this."

"Come on, you gorgeous hunk of woman, you!" Alec linked arms with her.

There was going to be open-air dancing after dark. He could hardly wait.

Ruth and Sammy took their time going round. Right from the first day Ruth had admired the Women of Empire Pavilion with its orange sunblinds, its fluttering pennants, its girdle of scarlet geraniums and pale forget-me-nots, its handful of pink lilies in the lily pond. To please her, Sammy went round the building with her yet again.

Ruth also liked the Keep Fit Pavilion run by the National Fitness Council for Scotland.

There had been quite a *furor* over that particular pavilion at first. Three eight-feet-high photographs of nude female statues had been a feature of the place, on mirror panels at the back of an open-air stage.

Indignant complaints were made about showing female figures and quite a battle raged as a result. Eventually a compromise decision was reached. The promoters of the pavilion decided that nude female figures, even though they were merely photographs of statues, were not quite the thing for the general public. They could, however, be shown discreetly in a more inconspicuous corner. And until they could be moved they were screened off from public gaze.

Ruth and Sammy had a last look at the two Scottish pavilions, one telling of the old Scotland of history and romance, the other showing the questing new life of Highlands and Lowlands.

They took the lift to the top balcony of the great steel

Tower of Empire on Bellahouston Hill and stared proudly down at the Empire spreading below in miniature but in miniature that was majestic in scale.

Good old Scotland! Sammy thought.

The clachan was their next stop. Ruth loved the little highland village. He preferred the Palace of Engineering although the clachan, tucked away on its own and separated from the rest of the park by trees, had an almost magical charm. Its rough shingled walks, its sedge grass, its crooked burn, its loch, and its kilted piper pacing its banks playing Scottish airs, was enough to catch at any Scottish heart, even one that preferred to live in a Scottish city.

In the thatched, whitewashed cottage with the plaque boasting "Highland Home Industries", Ruth lifted one of the heavy walking-sticks topped by the traditional shepherd's crook. "This would be a good gift for your father."

"Put it down!" Sammy's voice crackled with anger at her for spoiling a pleasant hour. "If he wants another stick, he can buy it for himself."

"All right."

Ruth pouted her lips a little as she put the stick back. To her, Hodge Hunter was only the man she saw for herself in the present. Sammy had never discussed his father with her. She must see, of course, that his father was a bully. She must despise him. She had quarrelled with him more than once, given up abominable cheek, yet the dislike she professed never seemed to run very deep.

Sometimes she even said things like: "Your father must have been a fine figure of a man in his uniform, Sammy!"

Or: "I can see how he managed to get three wives. A woman likes a forceful virile kind of man!"

"Forceful! Virile!" he'd spat in disgust. "He's already killed two of them. The one he's got now is maybe trying her best to hang on but have you had a good look at her lately? He's going to succeed in murdering her as well."

"Oh, now, Sammy." She had actually laughed. "Isn't

that going a bit far, love? The first one died in childbirth, and you never knew her. Your own mother had a heart condition, hadn't she?"

"He killed them both. He killed them," he insisted.

"All right, love. All right."

She tried to soothe him but he could see she did not understand.

He wanted so much to explain, but where could he start? To justify his attitude to his father would mean the raking over of too many painful years.

His brows pulled down, his eyes glittered and his jaw set with stubbornness.

Did killing only mean a dagger in the back, a bullet in the brain or poison in the belly? No, there were far more agonising, far more long-drawn-out, more subtle ways to kill. The murderer who used the subtle methods never reached a court of so-called justice.

His father was a murderer all right. He would never forget his mother's last heart attack, and now he was watching the slow disintegration of another victim.

Yet his father was a much respected member of the community. He had had a splendid record in the army. He was an elder in the church. Oh, the irony to watch him, straight-backed and pious at church every Sunday. His friends included ministers, school teachers and upright ex-army men with medals and courageous forays to boast of.

How often he had listened to these stories, recounted over glasses of whisky, noisy laughter and hearty camaraderie, in the Balornock front parlour.

Listened and hated until he had been sick.

They left the clachan in strained unhappy silence. A horrible thought was growing in his mind.

Did Ruth like his father? Could it be that she admired him? Little incidents flicked across his consciousness, odd glances from Ruth's dark eyes, the way she laughed at his father's jokes or the coy way she had of reprimanding him if she thought his stories were vulgar, the heightened self-consciousness in the way she walked in his presence or sat or moved her hands or tilted her head.

The horror grew.

"I'm sorry, love," Ruth said at last. "I know how you feel!"

But she didn't.

Chapter Ten

"May the good Lord forgive him!" Catriona's mother shook her head. "The man's not only wicked, he's stark raving mad!"

Catriona had a feeling that for once her mother might be right. The birth was only a matter of a few weeks away and Melvin was insisting that she must accompany him to the last day of the Exhibition.

As he was always telling her he believed in being a good family man and would never dream of going anywhere on his own. She tried to persuade him just to take Fergus along with him this time but without the slightest success.

"You know you want to go," he kept assuring her. "There's a massed pipe band parade and an anti-aircraft display. Planes are going to be coming across every ten minutes or so from Renfrew. It'll be marvellous. You'll love it!"

She could not imagine anything she would loathe more at this particular moment than the exhausting din of pipes and guns and planes.

Then there was the weather to contend with. Surely this had been the wettest summer for years!

"It's not a case of not wanting to go, Melvin." She made yet another attempt to make him see reason. "I'm just not able to trail around that Exhibition again."

"Nonsense! There's nothing special about being pregnant It's not an illness . . . . "

"Oh, all right, all right!" she hastily capitulated, putting her hands up to her ears and squeezing her eyes tight shut.

"Don't tell me how and where any more animals drop their young, or I'll scream."

He had been happy then, happy to be the good husband and father, taking his wife and son for a special treat.

She hated him as they set out for the Exhibition. Hatred battered inside her, hysterical for release, locked in and denied expression because of her need to lean on his arm for support, and to wheedle him for lifts on the autobuses, or reviving cups of tea, or to search for toilets.

"If you wouldn't drink so much, you fool," he told her angrily, "you wouldn't keep wanting to pee!"

"Sh-sh!" she miserably hushed him, her cheeks crimson with embarrassment. "People will hear!"

"So what! Everybody's got to pee at some time or other! It's only you that goes to extremes!"

"You're awful!" she hissed. "Awful!"

"Awful? What do you mean—awful? I don't pee all the time!"

"Stop saying that word!"

"What word?"

Frantic with desperation, she struggled to quicken her pace, at the same time changing the subject.

"Listen, Fergus! Look! There's the pipers!"

A mass of swaggering swinging tartan, disdainfully ignoring the squelching mud underfoot, racketed along, sparking the air with patriotic energy. Young folk pranced in front of and behind it, delighted with the sight and sound.

The child's eyes grew large and round, like baubles on a Christmas tree and he stamped up and down wildly clapping his hands.

Melvin laughed and cocked his head.

"He's having a grand time, eh?"

It was on the tip of her tongue to tell him that Fergus was over-excited but she bit the words down. The slightest criticism of the boy provoked his anger and indignation, and she had no wish and no energy for any more arguments.

66

They had waited in an enormous crush of people to get into the park, queued in fact for everything, and stood for what seemed a lifetime for a reviving high tea.

Buying a meal or even a cup of tea was an expense and a luxury that Melvin seldom indulged in and she had needed the rest and the food so much. Nothing in the future could ever compete with the utter joy of this.

By the time they had made their way to the anti-aircraft display the park was encased by a black night sky. The Exhibition sparkled in the darkness, a dancing fairyland of colour, the buildings caught in a flashing network of lights.

Despite the mud, people in raincoats and headscarfs and wellington boots were jostling and bumping together, singing at the pitch of their voices and dancing The Lambeth Walk.

"Any time you're Lambeth way,
Any evening, any day,
You'll find us all . . .
Doing the Lambeth Walk, oi!!"

Crowds were getting denser and the rain, now bucketing down, only served to increase their determination to have a riotous good time.

There was a wildness of spirit about the vast throng, a reckless abandon. It was as if the world were ending at midnight with the Exhibition, and they would never be able to enjoy themselves again.

Catriona began to feel frightened.

"Can't we go home now, Melvin?"

"Don't be daft."

"I'm tired."

The understatement of the world, she thought. She felt so exhausted she could barely speak. Every bone, every muscle, every organ in her body throbbed. She longed to stop moving; she had wistful dreams of a barrow or something, anything, on wheels to run along underneath her heavy belly to support it. She shuffled along, flat-footed, wide-legged in a daze of fatigue, caught in the centre, pushed this way and that by a mass of over three hundred and sixty-four thousand people.

"We'd never get out of here before midnight," Melvin said. "Not through this mob, not even if we wanted to."

The baby kicked and churned and protested inside her.

"Oh, Melvin!"

She tried to lean against him but he was lifting Fergus up into his arms.

"You're tired too, son, aren't you, eh? But you're not complaining. You want to see the guns and the planes, don't you? So does your mammy. She wants to see them, all right."

"I don't like guns. Melvin, I hate guns!"

Her voice was flattened by the roar of the anti-aircraft guns of the army mobile section.

She stared through tears like a drowning man gazing through a deep undulating sea. She was beyond caring what anyone thought, or what she must look like.

Rain smacked down, making her headscarf a limp rag and her hair a dripping net across her face. Her voluminous coat clung stickily, outlining every bulging curve of breast, buttock and abdomen.

She wept loudly but nobody heard.

Automatics roared, spat flames and shook the trees and buildings. Searchlights, long and powerful, criss-crossed to and fro, blue across the black sky. A plane zoomed off into the night out of range and started the big guns booming again.

Behind the guns were anti-aircraft experts with height-finding, predicting, and sound-recording apparatus. An officer shouted brisk orders.

Then the searchlights picked out another plane flying high above the tower and simultaneously more guns blasted into action.

People had stopped trying to move and just stood making

nearly two hundred acres of Bellahouston Park a solid block of humanity.

Catriona was too dazed to appreciate when the guns stopped, but gradually she became aware that a roar of voices had taken their place.

People grabbed hands, the park swayed.

"For auld lang syne, m'dear,
For auld lang syne,
We'll take a cup of kindness yet,
For the sake of auld lang syne."

The swaying heaved, quickened, jerked. Screams and laughter shot about like machine-gun bullets.

"So – here's – a – hand – my – trusty – freend,
And – here's – a hand – o' – mine.
We'll – meet – again – some – other – time,
For – the – sake – of – Auld – Lang – Syne !"

Then, from every corner of the park "God save the King" thundered out.

It was nearly midnight. The lights in the Tower of Empire went out and the searchlights concentrated on the top of the tower where the Exhibition flag, the proud lion of Scotland, was being slowly lowered.

Then dramatically, unexpectedly a voice came echoing across the hundred microphones from every corner of the ground.

"The spirit of the Exhibition greets you," boomed the voice. "I am no individual. I am composed of all those who have contributed to its success.

"I express to all who have made me, to all who have entered me, gratitude for their parts in me.

"I die tonight. May memories of me abide in your hearts."

In silence the crowd looked up while the strokes of Big Ben donged the hour and the flag slipped slowly down. It disappeared behind the wall of the top balcony of the tower and the Empire Exhibition was officially over.

It was the essence of Scotland that burst into one last

song to the many thousands of visitors who had come from all over the world to visit their friendly city.

"Will ye no come back again," Glasgow bawled heaven wards. "Will ye no come ba–a–ack again?"

Then began the great exodus. It looked as if three international football matches were all coming out at once.

"What a night!" Melvin enthused, still with Fergus in his long, muscly arms. "I bet you're glad you came. I knew you wouldn't want to miss it."

Catriona kept silent. She had a tight grip of his coat-tail as they jostled towards one of the exits along with the rest of the crowd and her whole concentration was on keeping hold of him so that he could clear a path for her and get her safely home.

Pain screwed her. Delirium fizzling up like champagne. Clinging to the coat-tail, holding it up, praying. Pain throttling. Head to one side, nostrils panicking.

Going away. At ease. Easy now. Easy now. Easy.

No one else in the world. Alone in a lonely place. Fighting for existence. A wedding ring clamping round guts.

A broad gold band, strangling, tightening.

Relax, the magazines said. Take lovely deep breaths and relax, you lucky, lucky mothers-to-be. One – two – three!

Who is the editor? Who is she? A man is the editor, he – he – he!

She did not recognise Dessie Street off the Main Road where cranes and ships towered up over the walls of the Benlin yards.

Leerie, leerie, licht the lamps,
Long legs and crooked shanks.

The shop at the corner had the blinds drawn down.

The blinds drawn down.

The blinds drawn down.

Gaslight wavered and flung deep shadows down the back close.

The spiral stairs wound round and round.

70

Round and round. Round and round.

She sank to her knees at the foot of them.

Oh, my God! Her lips puttered out with pain as she nursed herself.

Oh, my Jesus!

"The thing that puzzles me," she said, "is how a big baby is going to come out such a wee hole!"

The spiral stairs went up and down.

Up and down.

Up and down.

Way up high.

She was floating, quickly, hurriedly.

In through the front door, across the hall, into the bedroom.

Bed.

Oh, how good God was to her.

Thank you, God! Thank you, God!

The wedding ring was destroying her.

She fought it.

She tried to relax to please it.

She said she was sorry.

She cursed it.

She said she was sorry again.

And again. And again.

Yet it kept unbelievably contracting, crunching smaller and smaller with herself inside it not knowing what to do, or what could possibly happen next.

Until she knew that she could not stand any more or no more pain could ever be any worse.

It was then that agony leapt to new heights.

"Jesus!" she screamed high. Higher and higher. "Jesus!"

Then gradually she came back to the world again.

She felt the bed soft beneath her.

She saw the bedroom ceiling.

She knew she had experienced childbirth.

She told herself: Damn the women's magazines and all the romances in the world—don't you ever, ever forget this, girl. Don't you allow yourself to be conned into this ever again.

There was something soft, something making a strange cruchling sound against her. Utterly exhausted, she struggled to raise her head a little and peer down.

A red rubbery figure was sitting between her legs, tiny arms stuck out at each side and shiny matted head lolling helplessly.

Mrs Jackson was rubbing its back, then she suddenly grabbed it, held it upside down and gave it a resounding smack.

The cry echoed in Catriona's heart. With one last effort, she lifted, and held out her arms.

Chapter Eleven

The lights of Glasgow twinkling. Light beaming from shop windows and cinema doors. Neon sparkling high, winking busily. Trams and buses, bright yellow, swooping. Everywhere shimmery light.

Alec never forgot the moment he and Madge came back out of the cinema and found that Glasgow had disappeared. There was only darkness.

Neither spoke for a minute, but stood staring at eerie blackness, skin contracting, hair rising.

Glasgow, second city of Britain, home of over a million souls, lay as dark and quiet as a wayside hamlet. Not a single light anywhere. Tram-cars and buses creeping through the black canyons of the streets without one spark of illumination. Shops, cinemas, theatres, restaurants, houses, invisible behind blinded windows.

Only little obscured crosses of traffic signals and the dimmed warnings of other traffic direction signs hung in the blackness like miniature moonbeams.

People waited quietly and patiently in crowds at the tram and bus stops to get home.

Arms linked, fingers entwined, Madge and Alec toed their way cautiously along until they found their car stop.

They could not see if it was their own tram that came forward like a shadow to the stopping place but out of the darkness they heard the conductor's voice.

"Springburn!"

"Is it war, then?" Madge asked when they had found seats.

"Naw," he said. "No yet."

Alec chuckled and gave a match to his wife to hold while he searched for their fares.

"One thing's for sure. The courting couples will like this. Extra cuddles all round tonight!"

"Got yer call-up papers?"

Working in darkness seemed to have proved the last straw for the conductor, whose ghostly face was a bleak mask of depression.

"Go for the old medical tomorrow," Alec told him.

"Well, I hope ye pass awright."

"You must be joking," Alec laughed, lighting up a cigarette. "I'm praying I've got flat feet, ulcers, anaemia, and my intelligence is double-sub-normal."

The conductor sighed.

"If yer warm, yer in!"

"He's applying for a postponement," Madge said, pride lifting her voice. "On the grounds of exceptional hardship —because of me."

"You wouldn't be any hardship to me, hen!"

Madge enjoyed a hearty laugh.

"It's the weans. There's six now. Two sets of twins!"

"You'll never get off with that. Some folks have ten and more. Ah know a wumman down our street, so help ma boab, she's got twenty! There would be no Glasga fellas in the forces at all if you could get off with that!"

Alec blew out smoke and put an arm round Madge's shoulders.

"The wife's never been the same since the last two. Breech births, the twins were. Terrible, wasn't it, Madge?"

Madge gave another whoop of laughter.

"God, don't remind me! Talk about exceptional hardship!"

"Aw, well, anyways. The best o' luck to you, mate."

Stumbling, groping and cursing, the conductor disappeared upstairs.

The tram crawled cautiously, and Alec impatiently kept count of the stops.

"This one's ours, hen," he nudged Madge at last. "Watch your big feet getting off!"

"They'll have to do something about this," Madge giggled as she fingered her way along the shops and round the corner into Cowlairs Road.

"About this?"

"Get off!"

"Let's see your headlamps before you cross the road, hen."

"Stop being daft and hold my hand."

"I'll hold anything you want, gorgeous."

"Alec, I nearly tripped and broke my neck there. Keep a hold of me, I said!"

The walls of the pend dripped to the touch and stank fustily.

A cat miaowed past.

Madge's laughter bounced around and kept echoing back to her.

"You couldn't mistake this place!"

"My little grey home in the west."

"North!" Madge interrupted.

"Home, home on the range," he loudly belted out in mock drunkenness. "Where seldom is heard—a discouraging word, and the skies are not—cloudy all day!"

They staggered hilariously up the outside stairs, into the close, then up the hollow-beat wooden stairs to their door on the first landing.

Mrs Jackson's agitation clamped on to them and dragged them inside. A twitch was dancing around her eye.

"Thank God you're safe back."

"How did the bonny wee wean-minder get on, eh?"

Alec chucked her under the chin before collapsing back in the horsehair sofa in the kitchen and draping himself across it.

"I'll never get back to Clydend tonight, Alec. What'll I do, son?"

"Stay here! She's welcome to stay here, isn't she, Madge?"

"Och, of course! Sit down here, hen. I'm going to make a cup of tea."

"But my work. Oh, dear, dear."

"Relax, Ma," Alec advised. "It'll still be there tomorrow."

"But will *we*, son? Will we?"

Madge shouted with laughter.

"What's to stop us, for God's sake."

Mrs Jackson came very close as if Madge had gone deaf. "What's to stop us? What's to stop us? Any minute there's going to be a war. The last one was bad enough but this time there's going to be air-raids. You should do what your man tells you and evacuate yourself and the weans."

"I don't want to leave Alec, and anyway, Ma, I don't feel able to go stravaiging away with thousands of weans. Puddling along with my own mob from day to day's bad enough."

"She won't listen to me, Ma. I keep telling her it's for her own good."

"You can shove two or three of them in the pram and there's always somebody would help. Somebody would help. Anyway, poor Alec is going to be called up."

"He's trying for a postponement."

"That poor lad will have to go. They won't listen to him. They never listened to his father." Mrs Jackson's mouth went into a sudden grotesque paroxysm. She fought a battle with it and won. "The least you can do is see that the weans are kept safe."

"Ma's right, hen. I keep telling you. And you know what it said in the papers—Springburn's one of the bull's-eye areas."

Mrs Jackson began wringing hands that plopped with sweat.

"You're smack in the middle of all these works."

"You needn't talk." Madge grinned round as she splashed water in the teapot. "Dessie Street. At the docks?"

"Me being another bull's-eye doesn't help the weans. If

you think anything of these weans—you'll evacuate them."

"Och, poor wee buggers. I should, shouldn't I!"

"And the quicker the better if you don't want them blown to smithereens!"

"Och, all right, then."

Alec lit up another cigarette and accepted a cup of tea.

"That's my girl! What's the latest from Dessie Street, Ma?"

"Up the close, you mean?"

"Uh—huh."

His mother sat down beside him on the sofa and stirred vigorously at her cup. "Wait a minute now. There's eh . . . There's eh . . . " Blotchy patches of red appeared on her face. "Oh aye!" She gasped with the sudden relief of remembering. "You know Tam McGuffie?"

"The wee white-haired baker?"

"Yes, he and his wife and daughter live next door to Catriona MacNair." She leaned forward as if imparting a secret. "His father's moving in with him."

Alec chuckled.

"What's he called? Methuselah?"

"He's well over eighty and as deaf as a post. You know Catriona? Well, her father-in-law's coming to live with her too."

Madge poked the fire into life before settling down with her cup.

"Is that that wee blondie one who was expecting at the same time as me?"

"That's the one. I delivered the wean. What a night that was. I'll never forget it. A nice big wean she had though. Did you no see him in his pram one day? Andrew, she calls him. A nice wee lassie she is, Catriona."

Alec winked. "A right wee beauty as well!"

"Here, you!" Madge warned. "You keep away from her."

Mrs Jackson's mouth quivered again.

"Keep away? The poor lad's not going to have any

option. They'll take him away, I'm telling you, Madge. They won't listen about any postponement."

"It's great when you think of it." Alec shook his head. "I've never even met a ruddy German in my life!"

"Och, I know," Madge sympathised. "It's a damn shame All of them politicians should be put in a field and told to get on with it."

"What a thought!" Alec grinned.

Laughter made Madge splutter her tea.

"You've got a mind like a sewer. Fight, I mean. If they want a fight they should bloody well fight it out between themselves."

"They won't, though. Trust them," Mrs Jackson said bitterly. "They'll have that poor lad, that's for sure! They'll have him."

"Shut up, Ma!" Alec's good-humoured voice had the beginnings of an edge to it. "You're making me feel I've one foot in the grave already."

Madge put down her cup and stared in inarticulate distress.

"Don't worry, hen." Alec blew her a kiss. "The Jerries will never be able to run fast enough to catch up with me."

"Aye, son, you just take good care of yourself. You're a good lad. I couldn't stand you getting shot to pieces like your father."

"Ma, I couldn't stand it either, so will you shut up! You're scaring me rigid!"

"It's terrible to be a man, so it is!" Madge said. "Pack it in, Ma. Let's get to bed. Where do you want to sleep, hen?"

"I'll just slip in beside the weans."

Mrs Jackson nodded towards the high hole-in-the-wall bed behind the sofa where Agnes, Sadie and Hector sprawled in various poses of sleep. The three younger children were divided between prams over in front of the coalbunker and the cot through in the room.

"Better you than me!" Madge sent a peal of laughter

78

ceilingwards. "Them wee middens kick like horses. Do you want to go through and use the throne, hen?"

The throne was an old pail kept in a curtained recess in the room and used on cold nights to save going outside to the icy lavatory in the yard.

Mrs Jackson shook her frizzy head, her eyes still twitching anxiously at her son.

"No, away you go."

"I'll find you a nighty."

"No, no. I'll be fine in my vest and knickers for one night. If only that was the only thing I'd to worry about!"

"Well, if we didn't know there was a war in the offing before," Alec said, later in bed, "We know it now!"

Madge cuddled close to him.

"Och, Alec."

"What, hen?"

"What do they need you for? You're an insurance man."

"Maybe they need a policy!"

He could not be sure whether Madge had started to laugh or cry against his chest. She was a big girl and she was making the bed rock and bounce. He laughed, just to be on the safe side.

Chapter Twelve

Melvin swelled with rage. His eyes bulged and blotches of colour stained his cheeks. Catriona had never seen him so angry.

"That settles it!" He hitched back his shoulders and flexed his muscles. "I'm going to join up!"

She stared at him. Events were moving too fast for her comprehension.

The Prime Minister's broadcast still trumpeted solemnly in her mind like the heralding of doom:

"I am speaking to you from the Cabinet Room at 10 Downing Street.

"This morning the British Ambassador in Berlin handed the German Government an official note stating that unless we heard from them by eleven o'clock that they were prepared at once to withdraw their troops from Poland, a state of war would exist between us.

"I have to tell you that no such undertaking has been received and that consequently this country is at war with Germany . . ."

Then there was the terrible shock about Wee Eck the halfer. Wee Eck had worked as an apprentice-baker at MacNair's for years until recently when he had taken his cheeky grin and freckly face off to sea as a steward on a ship called the *Athenia*.

Incredible that cheerful, hard-working Wee Eck was dead. She could not accept it. Her mind clung tenaciously to the belief that there must be some sort of justice, order and fairness in the world. God and the powers that be only punished the wicked. The wicked suffered varying degrees of hell on earth according to their sins. Then came the final judgement day when every deed, every thought had to be accounted for and the judgement was either acquittal to the safety of heavenly regions or damnation in the fires of eternal hell.

She could well imagine herself destined for the torments of the abyss, but to believe that Wee Eck had done anything to warrant the terrors of death by drowning was completely beyond her.

The Donaldson Atlantic liner *Athenia* had been torpedoed and sunk without warning two hundred and fifty miles west of Donegal. Bound from Glasgow to New York, she was carrying fourteen hundred passengers. Radio messages from the sinking ship brought British destroyers full speed to the spot and passengers had also been picked up by a Norwegian vessel and a Swedish yacht.

Most of the survivors were landed at Galway and Greenock, many of them wounded or suffering from shock, but Wee Eck had been one of the hundred and twenty-eight killed.

"Joining up?" Catriona echoed.

"That's what I said."

"But what about your work and me and the children?"

"Don't be so selfish. You ought to be ashamed of yourself. At a time like this King and country comes first. Anyway there's Baldy—he's a good foreman and there's your father and Tam and Sandy McNulty. The army wouldn't give any of that lot a second look. Baldy's no use for anything except the bakery since they hanged his wife. Your father's got his ulcer and his dermatitis and everybody knows about old Sandy's feet. No, it's men like me they need in the army."

He stripped off his shirt to admire his bulging muscles in the sideboard mirror. Gripping his wrists, he grunted, wrenched himself this way and that and swelled himself up to grotesque proportions.

"Look at that neck! Look at those shoulders!" His moustache puffed. "Have you ever seen triceps like that? Good job I asked the old man to come and stay."

Jerking both arms up, elbows bent, fists clenched, as if he were about to punch himself in the ears, he forced his stomach muscles to do a circular rhythmic dance.

"The army won't have seen many men with muscle control like that."

Catriona watched hypnotised, as each muscle in his body in turn performed its cocky, bouncing pirouette. She could never credit how he managed to do this amazing trick of sorting out all his muscles and making them work separately.

In the privacy of the bathroom, she had tried to make her soft white body emulate his, but without the slightest success. The frustration of not being able to find any muscles at all nearly reduced her to tears. The only things she could jiggle were her small breasts and she managed that only when she jumped up and down.

"He'll keep on eye on things."

"Who'll keep an eye on what?"

"My father. He's not that old. Only there was no sense in him wasting money on a woman to do his house over there and cook his food for him."

"Who's going to keep an eye on him?"

"What do you mean, who's going to keep an eye on him?"

"You said he was drinking too much."

"I said nothing of the kind." Melvin stopped exercising and glared indignantly at her. "He likes a wee glass after he stops work at night. It washes away the flour."

"Your father may be the master baker but he's never baked for years."

The unfairness of Melvin's having insisted the old man lived with them, without either discussion or consultation with her, was something for which she would never forgive him.

"Are you insinuating that my father doesn't work hard?" Melvin's voice loudened as it climbed up the ladder of incredulity. "He's downstairs working now while you're lazing there on your backside!"

"My father worked all night with flour filling in his nose and mouth and hair."

"What do you mean—your father worked all night? *I* worked all night."

"It's different when my father takes a drink, though!"

Her voice held a bitterness that encompassed far more than what she said.

He came over and pushed his face down close to hers, enveloping her in a suffocating smell of onions and sweat.

"Your father can drink himself to death for all I care!"

Daggers of defiance aimed from her eyes to his.

"Oh, I know you don't care. You don't care about anything!"

She would like to have added "except yourself" but had not enough nerve.

Melvin straightened, bulged his eyes heavenwards and spread out his palms.

"Women! I've just said I'm going to join up and fight for my King and country!"

"Big man!" Catriona's mind twisted in sarcastic mimicry. "Big, brave, strong, kind, thoughtful, unselfish husband!"

"Oh, yes?" she said aloud.

"You don't believe me?"

Dutifully her gaze lowered, her voice smoothed out.

"Oh, yes, Melvin."

He scratched his moustache, then grinned.

"The Argyll and Sutherland Highlanders. I bet you'd be as proud as Punch to see me in a kilt. I've got marvellous legs for it, haven't I?"

"Yes, Melvin."

"Or the Black Watch. The lasses from Hell, the Huns called them in the first war. The Black Watch used to have a piper marching out in front, playing a stirring Scottish tune and behind him would come the men with fixed bayonets."

He laughed and puffed his chest up. "That would be a sight for the Huns. It must have scared them stiff. Can you imagine me in a kilt, eh?"

She could imagine him in the tartan all right, bulky shoulders, tree-trunk legs, kilts swishing smartly from side to side as he swaggered along.

"Well?"

"Yes, Melvin."

"The Black Watch or the Argylls! Or how about the Cameronians?"

"I'd better make the tea,"

"You're a fine one to talk about not caring. What regiment do you think?"

"It doesn't matter what I think." Catriona began setting the table. "Your father will be through for his tea in a minute."

The day he had told her that his father was coming to stay he had sat sucking his pipe, contented, at peace with himself and the world, as he announced:

"Oh, by the way, I've asked my father to move in with us. He needs someone to look after him in his dotage and there's no use paying two women."

Now, in the sharpness of her resentment, things that she had never noticed about the old man were becoming obvious. He was so mean, he never gave anyone any Christmas presents, not even his grandchildren.

"Just because I'm in business folk think I'm made of money," he would complain in his high nasal voice. "But I'm not. I've had to struggle all my life to keep body and soul together."

He could never resist a bargain and often bought clothes and boots from customers whose menfolk had died. Or if there were no deceased's clothing forthcoming when he needed it, he would go and haggle for a cut-price garment at the local pawn-shop. Nothing ever fitted. Collars never

84

matched his shirts and sagged forward over his straggle of beard. Suits of coarse, cheap material hung loose at his bottom and bulged at his knees. He always wore heavy boots and looked as if he were constantly on the point of walking out of them.

Every night at some time or other, he woke the baby with his clomp-clomp-clomping about.

But it was all Melvin's fault. The old man had not wanted to come.

"I see enough of Dessie Street when I work in the shop all day," he protested, but Melvin kept persuading him until eventually he talked the old man round by pointing out how much money he would save.

When Melvin broke the news, Catriona visualised the years ahead, the lack of privacy, the extra nagging at the children, the anxieties, the responsibilities, the heavy nursing when the old man became bedridden.

"You want to be the envy of the other women. I know you. So be sure you pick the best." Melvin scratched the surface of her attention. "The Argylls have the glengarry. Cocky looking it is with a couple of black ribbons streaming down the back, a red and white diced band with one line of the red squares joined to remind folk of the battle of Balaclava. You've heard of Balaclava?"

"No."

"You're a right one, you are! In Russia, you fool. The thin red line's famous."

"I remember now. It was a painting."

"A painting, be damned! It was a battle. The Argylls advanced in a great long line, all smart in their red tunics and kilts and white sporrans, bayonets at the ready." He thrust his fists forward and struck an aggressive pose as if he were threatening her with a bayonet. "There's nothing to beat the Jocks for tough fighting men. The salt of the earth, the Jocks are."

She had wanted to say, "You ought to have discussed this business about your father with me first. I don't know if I'm able to cope with him just now. I'm worried enough about the children."

But it was because of the children that she said nothing. She must not put Melvin in a bad mood just when she was working hard to butter him up to a receptive frame of mind in an effort to get his help and advice.

Fergus needed constant watching since Andrew was born. She dared not leave him alone with the baby and had to keep alert and watchful every minute the child was in the house.

She thanked God for school and the few hours of comparative peace it afforded her. Or the few occasions like this one, when Fergus had been persuaded to go out and play.

The peace was suddenly shattered by a piercing scream that made even Melvin jump. They both flew, jostling and pushing at each other to get into the bedroom.

The side of Andrew's cot was down and he was lying blue in the face, and choking, his woolly jersey rumpled up, his nappy at his ankles.

She reached him first and snatched him into the safety of her arms to cradle the soft rubber-milk flesh, and nurse it close.

"Sh . . . sh! Sh, sh! Mummy's wee lamb. It's all right. It's all right. Mummy's here! Sh . . . sh! Sh . . . sh!"

Fergus was standing very quietly beside the cot, a golliwog in his hands.

"How did you get in?" Melvin asked in surprise.

"Granda left the door open again, Daddy!"

"Feggie!" Andrew sobbed and pointed an accusing finger. "Feggie!"

Teethmarks were fast swelling into fiery lumps on the baby's thigh and spots of blood spurted.

Catriona felt sick.

"He had my golliwog," Fergus said.

"Did you give him that golliwog, Catriona?" Melvin shouted.

"Yes, but, Melvin . . . "

"Aw, shut up! You fool! Why did you have to find him Fergus's toy? He's got plenty of his own."

"I thought Fergus was too big for his golly now. I didn't know he still wanted it."

"Never mind, son." Melvin patted Fergus's head. "Tea's ready. Away and wash your hands."

"Melvin, I've been meaning to talk to you about Fergus," she said, when the child had gone. "I'm so worried. He does terrible things and I don't know how to handle him. The other day he was tormenting the baby and I just lost my temper and smacked and smacked him."

"You what?"

Melvin pushed his face close to hers, moustache spiking out, eyes bulging.

The baby had stopped crying and was sleepily hiccoughing against her shoulder. She wondered if she should lay him down in his cot again and hasten from the room in case Melvin's anger frightened him.

Or would it be better and safer to keep him rocking in her arms?

"I don't know what to do about Fergus."

"You want my advice, eh? Well, here's my advice. Don't you dare lift a finger to my son again or you're out on your ear." He pushed his face closer. "Is that understood? Has it penetrated that thick skull of yours? I'll throw you out of this house with only the clothes you have on your back. That's all you had when you came here and that's all you'll have when you leave."

He would take Andrew?

Catriona's eyes twitched about.

She stood perfectly still.

"Well?" Melvin roared. "Understood?"

"Yes, thank you," She managed politely.

Chapter Thirteen

"Sammy, you didn't!" Ruth's eyes guarded against panic.

"Why not? I do object!"

"You can't!"

His brows went down and his jaw set.

"Oh, can't I?"

"What will people think?"

"I don't care what people think."

"You do. You know you do. We both care. And all your brothers have joined up."

"They were always good soldiers." He said bitterly. "Theirs not to reason why, theirs but to do and die!"

"Sammy, your father!"

"What about my father?"

"Oh, now, please, love."

"Forget about my father."

"I can't forget about your father and neither can you."

"Why not? What's so special about him?"

"He was a regimental sergeant-major!"

"Oh, yes?"

"Sammy!"

"Ruth. I've registered as a conscientious objector and I'm going up before a tribunal. That's all there is to it."

"People will think you're a coward."

"Let them!"

Anger widened Ruth's eyes.

"No, I will not let them. You're not a coward."

He shrugged.

"What does it matter?"

"It matters a lot. I won't let them." Her voice weakened, became petulant like a child's. "It's not that I want you to go, Sammy. I hate the war. I don't even know what it's about. All I want is to have you with me in our nice wee house. We weren't doing anybody any harm. Just living our own nice quiet lives."

A burst of humourless laughter escaped from Sammy.

"A nice quiet life! We've had that from now on."

"But if you change your mind."

"It won't change the war."

"But, Sammy . . ."

"You can't have a nice quiet life during a war."

"Oh, I don't know?" She flashed back at him. "You seem to be making a jolly good try for one."

"I was prepared for that from other people. But not from you."

"I didn't mean it." Ruth stamped her foot. "I didn't mean it. I hate you for making me say that."

"I'm sorry."

"You can't be a conscientious objector."

"I must."

"Everybody will hate you." She stamped again, her face twisting in tears. "I can't bear it!"

He took her in his arms.

"As long as you don't hate me . . ."

"You always said you'd do anything for me." Her body squeezed provocatively against his. "Anything."

"I know."

"Well, don't be a conscientious objector. Please, Sammy. Please?"

"Ruth . . ."

"You could join a corps where you would just be doing office work the same as you're doing now."

"Ruth, you don't understand."

"Or the military police, like your father. Wouldn't he be pleased?"

He pushed her away.

"Oh, shut up!"

"Sammy!"

"The only connection I'll have with the military police is when they come to arrest me!"

"Don't talk like that."

"After the tribunal they'll come for me."

"And take you to the army?"

"Yes."

She pressed wheedlingly close again.

"Well, if you're going to be made to go in the end love, why cause all this fuss? Why bother with being a CO?"

A flush crept up from his neck and his voice began to tremble.

"I'll do nothing they say. I'll disobey every order. I'll refuse to put on the uniform. I'll have nothing to do with anything military. I hate them."

She stared in bewildered silence for a minute.

"You feel as strongly as this?"

"I hate them!"

"Well," she decided, "if that's how you feel, that's how I feel. But your father will be furious!"

He nodded.

"Ruth, you'd better go out. Go to the pictures or something."

"Go out? Now? Without you? Why? What do you mean?"

"He's coming."

"Your father?"

"I went up today, to get it over with—to tell him, but he wasn't in. I waited for a while but I knew you'd be getting worried so I left a note. He's bound to have read it by now. He'll come."

Ruth shrugged.

"Your conscience is your business. He has no right to interfere."

"I don't want you getting upset. You don't know what he's like."

"I'm not going anywhere without you." Her full lips pouted. "Imagine, me without you!"

She kissed him and he held her tightly and thought if nothing good ever happened to him again he would still consider himself a lucky man because of her.

"I think I'll go back," he said suddenly. "I don't want unpleasantness here." With his arm still encircling her shoulders, he surveyed the immaculate kitchen. "We've made a good job of this, haven't we?"

"It's just right."

"In good taste yet homely and comfortable."

"Everybody admires it."

"Happy, too. There's a feeling of happiness about it. That's your doing, Ruth."

"You're the one who's made me happy, love. Mum and Dad's place was never like this." She groaned. "All that crowd! Never any peace, any privacy, any security. I don't know how my mother stuck it."

"She was a fine-looking woman."

"I wished she'd lived just a little longer. Just to see me married and happy."

Sammy shook his head.

"Sixteen children and your mother and father in that room and kitchen. My God!"

"She liked nice things, you know." Ruth's eyes looked back and glimmered with amusement. "She used to keep a half set of china and a sugar bowl and a milk jug locked away in the room cupboard and only brought them out at New Year or at other very special times when we had visitors. I used to think that china was marvellous. We just used tinnys, you know, tin mugs and the milk out of the bottles and the sugar out of the bag." She leaned her head down on his shoulder. "Now I use china all the time and I've a crystal sugar and cream."

"If I had the money you would have better than this."

"Nothing could be better than this. I've everything I want here."

He kissed her on the brow and her gaze fluttered coyly up at him.

"Well, nearly everything."

He sighed.

"A child, you mean? We're barely out of our teens. We've plenty of time."

"We keep putting it off. Saving up for other things."

"The other things you wanted," he reminded her.

"I know, love, but I was thinking . . ."

"Don't worry, one day we'll get a wee house in Bishop-briggs with a patch of garden back and front."

"For the baby's pram?"

Already the scene was melting in her eyes.

He nodded.

"I could save up the deposit in two or three years."

"It would be a bit difficult here with a pram right enough. I'd never manage it up and down all these stairs."

"I wouldn't let you."

For a few minutes, surfing along on the tide of her enthusiasm, he had forgotten about the war and his father and been happy. Now, suddenly, there was a loud rapping at the door, and happiness scattered.

"Now, don't be upset, Ruth. Just keep calm. Blast! Blast! I ought to have gone back. I should never have given him the chance to come here."

"Sammy, love . . ."

"It's all right. It's all right. Don't get upset. Don't worry!"

"One of us had better open the door before he breaks it in."

"Now, don't you worry!"

"Sit down," she said. "I'll go."

He was grateful to her for giving him the chance of a minute or two on his own to arrange himself in a casual, relaxed pose on the chair facing the kitchen door. He took a slow, deep breath.

He meant to say nonchalantly, "Oh, it's you, Father! Did you get my note?"

But his father's eyes shrivelled him back to his childhood.
"You're a bloody coward!"
The silver-topped stick bayoneted out, cracked against Sammy's chest and doubled him up, rasping and red-eyed, clawing for breath.
"Leave him alone!"
Ruth rushed to his aid but was knocked aside.
Sammy rose from the chair still choking, but another blow reeled him back.
"You're a bloody coward!"
Hatred came pulsing to Sammy's rescue.
"Get out of my house."
"Och, the big brave man, is he? But not big enough or brave enough to fight for his King and country."
"Get out."
"I could make mincemeat of you, son. I didn't spend half a lifetime in the army without learning how to make mincemeat out of the likes of you."
Ruth clung to Sammy's arm, and he could feel her trembling.
"You heard what Sammy said."
"He hasn't said what I came to hear and I'm not leaving until he says it."
"If you're waiting to hear me tell you I'm going to join the army, you're wasting your time."
"Och, I've plenty of time, son."
"Mr Hunter," Ruth tried again. "If you don't leave us alone I'll go for the police."
"You just keep your stupid mouth shut, woman. We've always settled our own affairs inside the family. We've never needed anybody else."
"Oh, haven't we?" Bitterness weltered Sammy like a fire-hose shooting acid. "That's where you're wrong. Somebody should have locked you up in an asylum years ago."
Unexpectedly, the heavy-handled stick shot out again.
"Sammy!" Ruth's cry was panic-stricken.

From somewhere down a dark tunnel he managed to grab the stick and hang on, muscles straining as he heaved it towards the door, every now and again wrenching and twisting but still forcing his weight against his father with all the pent-up fury of years.

The door banged shut and he lay against it for a moment, his lungs hiccupping for air. Blood was rapidly spreading over his best white shirt and he stripped it off as he returned to the kitchen.

Ruth's face was all ink-black eyes and a white blotting paper skin.

"Oh, Sammy!"

"Bastards!" he said. "Bastards. All of them!"

Chapter Fourteen

Alec read the notice again.

" 'Parents should see that on the day of evacuation their children are equipped with the following: A gas mask. A change of underclothing. Night clothes. House shoes or rubber shoes. Spare stockings or socks. A toothbrush. A towel. A comb. Handkerchief. A warm coat or macintosh. A tin cup or mug.' Well, hen," he asked Madge, "have you got six of everything?"

Madge tucked her hair behind her ears and grinned at him. She was ready at the front door with the babies crushed together in the pram and Hector, Agnes and Sadie and Maisie hanging on to her coat-tails.

"Combs and toothbrushes would be no use to them." She indicated the babies, now christened William and Fiona. "Poor wee buggers! Toothless and hairless!"

"Well, come on, gorgeous, don't dilly-dally."

The grin still stuck on her freckled face but her eyes became worried.

"You're not just wanting to get rid of us, Alec?"

"Dope! If I wanted rid of you lot the best way would be to keep you here. The Jerries would soon blow you to kingdom come."

"But what about you?" Her smile disappeared. "You'll be here."

"Not as much as you and the weans would, hen. I'm collecting, on the move all day, and often at night, remember, and now I've to do this fire duty. I've enough on my plate without worrying about you, so come on! I'll see you to the school."

From early morning evacuees had been assembling at the schools in the evacuation areas where teachers and other harassed adults were endeavouring to make order out of chaos. Labels pinned to their lapels, gas masks slung over their shoulders and tin mugs tied to the gas masks; clutching coats, teddy bears and toys the children see-sawed between hysterical delight at the novelty of it all and the fearful dread of the unknown. They milled and crushed and pulled and pushed and giggled and waved good-bye and wept broken-heartedly.

Glasgow sprouted children as if an invisible Pied Piper was conjuring them up endlessly out of nowhere. They hustled down streets, packed buses and trams, and swelled stations and trains to bursting point.

Alec's mind boggled at the thought of so many unsuspecting country houses about to be forcibly invaded.

Billeting officers were empowered to serve house-holders with notice requiring them to provide accommodation for a certain number of evacuees and where actual rooms were commandeered, an offence was committed if they were not immediately vacated.

Failure to comply with the regulations could bring a fine of £50 or a three-months' prison sentence.

"My God, hen," Alec laughed. "And I thought I was the only one swelling the population."

Although Madge laughed, she looked disconcerted. William and Fiona whimpered and Maisie sucked her thumb and looked tired.

"Where are they all coming from, Alec?"

"God knows! But just you keep with the teachers or whoever's in charge. Do what they tell you. They're organising everything."

"Poor buggers! Better them than me."

"Well, it's time I was back at work, hen. I won't pay the rent standing here."

96

They had reached the gates of the school and small children and tall children, all lumpy with burdens and jaggy-cornered with gas mask containers, converged from every direction. Alec began to feel restless, hemmed in.

"I'll away then."

Madge automatically jiggled the handle of the pram about in an effort to rock and quieten William and Fiona.

"Remember and send me some money, Alec."

"The first weekend after you send me your address, hen, I'll be down to see you and bring you some."

Alec leaned closer to her and pinched her bottom. "I'll be saving up more than money for you, I'm warning you— so be prepared!"

She flung up a big toothy laugh and then gave each of the children leaning against her a jab towards him.

"Say cheerio to Daddy."

"I don't want to go away," Sadie wailed, and Agnes, Maisie and Hector took up the words like a fugue ending in unison with,

"Dad . . . dae!"

Madge laughed again.

"Och, well, at least I don't need to worry about them making a noise. No one's going to hear them in the middle of everybody else's racket."

Noise was attacking them from all sides and Alec's brains began to crash together like cymbals. He couldn't hear himself think.

Hastily he swung Sadie, Agnes, Hector and Maisie up into the air and kissed them. He dropped a kiss on William's and Fiona's cheeks, now hot and wet with the exertions of screaming. A quick kiss for Madge and he was backing away when, in an unexpected flurry of movement, she let go of the pram, rushed forward and grabbed hold of his jacket.

"Now, Madge," he laughed, inwardly groaning. "It's not like you to make a fool of yourself, hen."

She released him, tucked her hair behind her ears and

began bouncing the pram again, laughing with embarrassment.

"You never said you'd miss us."

"Gorgeous!" He blew her a kiss. 'I'll be miserable just living and waiting for that weekend."

Never before in his life had he been so glad to escape.

He was up to the top of his head in sound and knee deep in children, wading, struggling through them. He thought he would never get clear, never reach the cool dark quiet of his favourite pub with its newly-opened, wet-floor, disinfectant smell more pungent than the beer.

Once the pub had been successfully achieved he celebrated his freedom and new-found bachelorhood with a double whisky and a big golden frothing pint.

"Cheers!" he said, raising the whisky to everybody and nobody. He felt on top of the world.

War, he decided, had its advantages.

For the first time in years he felt really free. No anxieties about keeping the peace at home, no worries about Madge marching in on him either at the office or at somebody's house.

She had nerve, Madge—he had to give her credit. Old Madge would barge in where angels feared to tread and there was a streak of violence in her that had to be seen (or felt) to be believed. She looked harmless enough with that freckly face and those laughing blue eyes but she packed a wallop like the back legs of a horse. Not that he had ever been at the receiving end. But he had winced in sympathy a few times when she had dished out a black eye or a bloody nose to some of his female acquaintances.

Madge was loyal to him no matter what happened; all the same he often got the feeling he was teetering along on a tightrope and one day he would slip and fall. Life seemed more and more a series of narrow escapes.

Now, suddenly—freedom! Whistling cheerfully he returned to the street. He did not feel like working. The prospect of going home and making himself a meal did not appeal to him either, and he decided to take the rest of the day off to celebrate. First he would go over to his mother's in Clydend for a meal and while he was there try and get the chance to chat up the wee blondie who lived up the same close.

He had passed the time of day with her a few times already. The poor girl was sex-starved. She fluttered and flushed and became as excited as a child with Santa Claus if he even glanced in her direction. It was pathetic. Her man had always worked nights, of course, and now he had joined up.

A sex-starved wife and a crazy husband. It took all kinds to make a world.

Alec's mother was at home and welcomed him with unconcealed delight.

Blissfully unaware of the reason for his now more frequent visits she immediately began searching out the little titbits she saved up for such occasions.

"I've got a cake, son!" She came up close and gave him a conspiratorial nudge with a bony elbow. "Tipsy! Your favourite! Tipsy cake!"

He winked.

"Great, Ma!"

"And a few potatoes. I'll make chips. It won't take a minute, a few chips."

"Great, Ma!"

She would take ages. She was at the change of life he reckoned, and it affected her that way. She wandered aimlessly about, dropping whatever she touched, getting into mix-ups and forgetting where she had put everything from her corsets to her purse.

Restlessly, he strolled through to the room and stared down from the tiny attic window to the cobbled Dessie Street below.

Not every child had been moved to the safety of the countryside. Some still played with balls and skipping ropes, boys wrestled and punched, girls crawled along the pavement drawing peever beds with lumps of pipe-clay oblivious of their dangerous nearness to the docks across the main road and the high ships on stocks and other vessels crowding the river.

He returned to the kitchen lighting a cigarette. His mother was standing in the middle of the floor like a white-faced golliwog, her fingertips trembling against her mouth.

"This is my last fag, Ma," said Alec. "I think I'll run down for some."

"I was just trying to remember where I put the cake, son. A tipsy cake. I know I have it somewhere."

"Don't worry, Ma. I'm in no rush. Take your time, hen."

Her lips were like elastic, stretching, pursing, moving about.

Eventually she managed: "You're a good lad!"

Alec shut the front door and stood for a minute or two on the landing.

Careful does it, he thought. The little blondie downstairs was maybe desperate for it but women were strange, touchy creatures and she was stranger and touchier than most.

For months now he had been doing a verbal minuet with her and it was proving the oddest experience of his life.

He still could not be perfectly sure what to make of her but he suspected that somewhere inside this delicate little butterfly there were emotions just as strong as those more obvious in Ruth Hunter.

Up till recently, of course, she had always been afraid of her husband suddenly appearing, and jumped and fluttered at the slightest sound, but now that he was out of the picture things should be different.

Not that her old man would have been justified in raising an eyebrow at anything that had happened so far: a chance meeting or two on the stairs, a few laughs and talks at her door. He had spoken to her downstairs in the shop, and a couple of times they had met for longer periods at his mother's place, the girl's gold hair and radiant face lighting up the dark attic room.

Puffing at his cigarette and blowing smoke out in front of him he went down the stairs until he came to the door marked Melvin MacNair.

He gave his usual rat-tat-tat-tat-tat. Tat-tat!

As always Catriona peeped timidly round a crack, then opened the door slowly, cautiously.

"Hello there, gorgeous. How do you do it, eh?"

Her eyes smiled, fluttered down, shoulders and hands squeezed up to stifle giggles.

"Do what?"

"Look more beautiful every time I see you. Look at that hair."

Alec's hand went out to touch her hair and as usual she jerked back like a terrified doe. Only this time he was ready and his fingers reached and held, and wound round the soft silkiness.

"Anybody else in, hen?"

"No," she whispered, cringing as if he were striking her.

He chuckled. She was just standing there letting him play with her.

"Aren't you going to ask me in?"

"I'm here by myself. The children are at my mother's and my father-in-law's down in the shop."

"I've just come for six pennies for a sixpence for the gas. Ma was making me something to eat and her gas ring's gone out."

"Oh! Oh, yes, yes. Yes, of course."

The girl wriggled her head from under his hand and flew across the hall towards the kitchen.

He followed her into the house and quietly shut the door.

This was a lot different from his mother's poky place up under the rafters. There was a square room hall with various doors leading off it.

Polish was the keynote. The pungent waxy smell of it thickened the air. Everything was polished: even the walls, decorated with heavy embossed paper, shiny enough to see your face in. The doors, like the dark brown linoleum, gleamed and glittered, daring anyone to deface them.

Stepping-stones of little rugs were dotted here and there. With great care he stepped on them until he reached the room into which Catriona had fled.

It was an immaculate, highly polished kitchen with sparkling sink and sideboard, table and chairs.

Funny, he thought, Ruth Hunter's place was as posh and well kept as this but so much more comfortable and homely.

"Find any, gorgeous?"

She gave such a scream of terror at the unexpected sight of him that even he jumped.

"My God, hen!" He collapsed into one of the chairs by the fire, his hand on his chest. "You just about frightened the life out of me!"

The girl's eyes remained enormous but laughter gurgled in her throat, escaping from her mouth in jerky little bursts. She put a hand up to try and control it, looking uncertain, apologetic, as if she were afraid he might be angry with her for making a rude noise.

Alec grinned at her and shook his head.

"You're an awful wee lassie!"

The fear went out of her eyes and she lowered her gaze and giggled childishly, and Alec immediately saw his cue. Here was a real Peter Pan, a girl who had never grown up.

"Come over here!"

He pointed to the rug at his feet.

Obediently she came.

"Am I a friend of yours?" he asked, trying to sound stern.

"W–w–well I . . . I suppose you are."

"Didn't I carry your heavy message basket and your wean up the stairs for you the other day?"

"Yes, you're always very kind."

"Didn't my mother deliver your wean?"

"Oh, yes. Oh, she's been terribly kind."

"She's your friend?"

"Oh, yes, I don't know what I'd do without her."

"And I'm your friend?"

She nodded and smiled tentatively.

"Well?" he said, his eyes beginning to twinkle. "Don't you know how to treat friends?"

Worry cast a shadow over her face and she did not answer.

He leaned forward and caught hold of her hands.

"It's easy, hen, just be friendly!"

Chapter Fifteen

He pulled her on to his knees and into his arms before she had time to realise what was happening and for a few minutes he held her like a baby, rocking her, patting her. She stiffened at first as if she were going to struggle but it was only for an imperceptible moment, until she fell under the spell of the gentle rocking.

Alec stroked and played with her hair and when he looked down he saw that her eyes had closed.

His hand slid down over her blouse and found her small breast. Immediately her arms flew up to hug herself protectively.

"What's wrong?" he queried in aggrieved surprise as if she had offended him.

Her gaze shrank down.

"I'd better go and get the pennies for your mother."

"There's no hurry."

"I'd better go."

He smiled.

"I'm stronger than you, hen."

Before she could panic his mouth quietened her and he burrowed down into a more comfortable position to enjoy a long slow exploration, but she was trembling and shaking and shivering with such violence that his plan to proceed in a leisurely fashion had to be abandoned.

"No, please!" She struggled up for air. "Oh, please. Somebody might come in. What if somebody saw me?"

She wept broken-heartedly.

"Sh–sh!" He stroked her hair. "I don't want to upset you—just love you."

"Love me?" Immediately her gaze beseeched him. "You mean that?"

"Of course."

"You love me?"

"Adore you!"

"Is that the same as loving? Does that mean you care about me?"

"I love you. I really care about you. All right?"

"No . . . no!" She began to struggle again. "Somebody might see me!"

"Gorgeous, you're in an upstairs flat. Are you frightened a passing pigeon will keek in?"

"I couldn't bear it."

"Sh . . . sh . . . All right. All right." He lifted her up in his arms. "I'll take you anywhere you want to go."

He carried her out into the dark hall.

"Where's the bedroom?"

"Oh, no, please, please put me down."

"You know I love you, don't you?"

She shook her head, eyes wet and helpless.

"Well, gorgeous, I do!"

He let her slide down as he kissed her again.

"Come on," he urged. "What room?"

"No, somebody might see through the windows."

"We could draw the blinds."

"Everybody would know."

The situation was becoming ridiculous but he managed to keep his voice low.

"Here then? It's dark and there's no windows."

Furtively, fearfully she peered around.

"The doors are open."

"Not the front door. It's locked."

"The other doors."

"Sweetheart, we can shut them if it'll make you feel happy."

He kept his arm firmly around her as they went round the hall securing every door.

"All right now?"

Another fit of shivering took possession of her.

"Somebody could see through the letter-box."

With an effort, he controlled himself.

"If we open this cupboard and stand behind it, nobody could see, not even through the letter-box."

He manoeuvred her against the cupboard shelves.

"Anyway, it's pitch dark."

"It's important."

"What is, hen?"

"That I know for sure."

"Nobody can see."

"That you love me."

"I told you."

"Promise me you mean it."

"I promise."

"I want you to be perfectly honest. I need to feel sure."

So anxious was she in testing his sincerity and anxiously searching his eyes that she was unaware of his fingers deftly unbuttoning and baring her. But the moment the heat of their bodies came together she gave a strangled cry of surprise and began struggling and fighting.

"Sh . . . sh," he whispered. "Somebody will hear you."

At once she quietened and became motionless.

"Good girl," he rewarded her. "Good girl."

He took as long as he dared. After all, the old man was liable to come up from the shop and for all he knew her battle-axe of a mother might be due to arrive on the scene.

"Your father-in-law or your mother might come," he told her eventually. "I'd better go."

He allowed her to cling on to him and he kept his arm around her until they reached the outside door. He unlocked it, then disentangled himself.

"Thanks, hen. I'll see you again soon."

Her voice quavered out faint and high-pitched like an infant's.

"You won't tell anybody about me?"

"Don't be daft!"

He blew her a kiss before shutting the door and rapidly returning upstairs.

"I've got it all ready, son," his mother greeted him, with a flushed, triumphant face.

"Just a minute, Ma. Give me a minute, hen, there's something I'm bursting to do."

He staggered past her into the kitchen and collapsed full length on the sofa.

Laughter exploded up from his belly in jerks and swirls, madder and madder like a firework display. He writhed and clutched himself and flayed about shouting and howling.

"Are you feeling all right, son?"

Uncertainty tipped his mother's voice off balance.

He sat up, fished for a handkerchief and wiped tears of hilarity from his eyes.

"Great, Ma! What's for tea, hen? I'm starving."

She had committed adultery. She had committed adultery.

Catriona wandered back to the kitchen in a daze. Reaching a chair her legs tottered and gave way.

She had broken one of God's commandments.

All the sins that had harassed every year of her life faded into nothing compared with this—this monstrous wickedness.

To think that only an hour ago she had been sitting here alone believing herself to be dangerously near a suicidal level of worry.

Since Melvin had gone she had somehow lost her grip on life. Old Mr MacNair and her mother between them had taken the reins.

Her father-in-law was becoming more and more of a whiner, harping on continuously about everything from the rotten weather and bad-paying customers to stupid nyucks in the government who'd got everyone into another ruinous war.

If he was not wearing her nerves to threads of irritation with his complaining, he was depressing her with tales of disaster and death. He studied the evening paper's Deaths column with avid interest, often reading each announcement to her word for word, and had even indignantly complained on one occasion:

"There's only two deceaseds tonight!"

Apart from upsetting her, she felt sure the old man's conversation must have a bad effect on the children.

She confided in her mother and pleaded for advice, only to have the children promptly wrenched away from her.

"But, Mummy, you can't take them to stay at your place," she had protested in panic. "What will I do without them?"

"Oh, be quiet!" Her mother's face twisted in disgust. "I'm sick of your selfish whining. You're as bad as that man."

"It's not that Da means any harm. It's just he's getting old and . . . . "

"Oh, be quiet."

Her mother turned her attention back to Andrew, nursing him, smiling fondly at him, dandling him up and down.

"Granny's lovely wee pettilorums, wee lovey-dovey darling—yes!"

"Give Andrew to me, Mummy."

Feeling suddenly afraid, Catriona stuck out her hands.

"Please, I want him."

"You're a wicked, selfish girl. What do you care if this poor infant's buried alive."

"Buried alive?"

Her eyes were enormous.

"This is the most dangerous place in Glasgow. May God in his infinite mercy help and protect you."

"I want my baby."

Catriona made a grab at Andrew and tried to pull him

forcibly from the strong muscular arms, but was knocked back as Andrew let out a machine-gun panic of squeals.

"You wicked, wicked girl. Now look what you've done."

Her mother began pacing the floor, bouncing Andrew against her buxom chest.

"Never you mind that bad Mummy, lovey. Granny won't let that bad Mummy touch Granny's wee lovey again."

Following her mother about the room, trembling with agitation, Catriona repeated over and over again:

"I want my baby. I want my baby."

"Get out of my way," her mother commanded. "I'm taking these children to where they'll be safe and with the Good Lord's help properly looked after."

"I can look after them and they'll be as safe here as in Farmbank."

"Don't talk nonsense! There's only a council housing scheme in Farmbank. Why would the Germans want to bomb that? May God in His infinite mercy forgive you! You are putting your own selfish desires before the safety and well-being of these children. Come on, Fergus, you carry Granny's message bag."

She swung round again. "And you," she said, "had better pack a case with their things and bring it over to me at Farmbank after you've seen to the old man's tea tonight. I'm warning you, Catriona, God has His own way of working. He'll punish you for your wicked selfishness. Something terrible is going to happen to you or to someone you love."

She had determined to follow her mother and somehow snatch the children back again and this determination and the wicked selfishness of it had been churning around in her mind when she heard the unexpected rat-tat-tat at the door and Alec Jackson appeared.

Now she felt too afraid to face the children in case they might know what she had done and be ashamed of her. Her uncleanness was so abominable it was bound to be clearly visible to everyone's eyes.

Yet her ache for her baby tugged at her mercilessly. She loved and wanted Fergus too, but her feeling for him, try as she might, could never equal the acuteness, the exquisite pleasure-pain she experienced at the mere thought of Andrew.

She got up and began pacing the floor, desperate to run all the way to Farmbank and fight tooth and nail to get the children back, yet fearing that in her present shocked state she might do the wrong thing again, might go on heaping one dreadful sin upon another.

What if she did manage to bring Andrew back, and there was an air-raid and he was killed? She burst into tears and stood in the middle of the floor wiping messily at her face with the backs of her hands.

If loving meant really caring then she ought to care about the children, not herself, she ought to put them first.

She pressed her lips firmly together and breathed big jerky breaths.

Tea-time. Set the table. Clever girl.

For hours she wandered about the house trying to reassure herself. She longed for comfort. Not for Melvin's bullying voice, his harsh laugh, his heavy bull-body but for somebody who really cared about her.

Thoughts of Alec's gentleness relaxed her like an anaesthetic. Her hiccoughing breaths soothed and subsided. Alec would tell her what was best for the children.

It was late now and it was dark but she would go to him and he would make everything all right.

Her mind made up, she hurried to get her coat and find the tram-car that would carry her through the blacked-out city and to Alec's house in Springburn.

Chapter Sixteen

The Society of Friends, the Quakers, held Fellowship Meetings and mock tribunals for conscientious objectors, to prepare them for what was to come, to help them clarify their position in their own minds and to give them practice in answering questions.

The Quakers were a revelation to Sammy, surprising him first of all with their obvious lack of prejudice. Everyone was welcomed at the Meeting House by the same warm shake of the hand and the same cheerful acceptance. It obviously made no difference if one was a Quaker, a Plymouth or any other kind of Brother, a Jehovah's Witness, an Independent Labour Party man, a Christadelphian, a Freethinker, a Christian Scientist, a Methodist, a Humanist, an atheist.

Sammy discovered that the Meeting House, a converted terrace house near Charing Cross, had its own library and before the mock tribunal started he had a browse through some of the books, and a few shy words with a Quaker called John Haddington, who came into the room to stand puffing at a pipe and heating his coat-tails at the fire.

The whole place was so unlike a normal church, both in appearance and in practice, that Sammy was quite intrigued. From what he had read and been told about them, he discovered Quakers believed that everyone, including women—who had enjoyed absolute equality with men right from the time of the founder George Fox— were part of the ministry. Therefore anyone could get up during meeting for worship and voice a prayer or anything he might feel moved to say.

Perhaps someone might recite a poem that had comforted or inspired him.

Another might stand up and give a few brief words on a special event.

After a silence another Friend might comment on what the original speaker had said, and so with respectful, thoughtful silences in between each speech, a little discussion might arise, a tentative spiritual probing.

Or the hour-long meeting might be held in unbroken quiet, a spiritual waiting in which the clamour of daily life was stilled. At the end of the hour notices would be read out, including the announcement that coffee was being served upstairs and all visitors would be most welcome.

"Coffee time's the best time!" John Haddington amused Sammy with his candour. "We have a rare old talk then and thoroughly enjoy ourselves."

As far back as Sammy could remember he had always had a church connection but it had never had much to do with enjoyment.

He had been marched to Sunday School and Bible Class. Eventually he had become a church member. The church was a background, part of the pattern of his life. Now he and Ruth attended church together.

But he had never given religion the same serious thought as he had other subjects. Ever since his childhood he had been an avid reader, and Ruth and he enjoyed going to the library twice or three times a week to change their books, but he had never bothered much with the shelves marked Religion.

His church membership was a prestige symbol, a sign of respectability more than anything else. It pleased Ruth if they dressed in their best and set out arm in arm for church on a Sunday. Their church connection gave them a place in the community and a set of decent standards to live by.

Here at Quaker Meeting House he sensed with deep

inward surprise that there might be something beyond and above this.

He sat self-consciously through the Fellowship Meeting and mock tribunal yet warming with gratitude for the practical help the Quakers, and John Haddington in particular, were giving him.

He had been completely in the dark about the coming tribunal; now, thanks to the Friends, he had some idea of what to expect, and could begin to prepare himself for the ordeal. He intensified his reading, taking pages and pages of notes to make his point on the day.

He had condensed the notes and rewritten them in a neat hand on a series of little cards that would fit in his wallet. He had muttered his arguments as he dressed, he had tried them out on Ruth until at last she asked worriedly, "Do you think you should learn all this, love? You might never get the chance to say it."

"But this is the basis of my objection," he protested irritably. "The point of these tribunals is to find out who really has a conscientious objection."

"I know."

She kissed him on the brow, then on the eyes, then on the mouth.

"Don't lose your temper. Especially at the tribunal. That's what you'll have to remember more than anything else."

The day had come, and Ruth was helping him as only she could. She took extra care in the washing and ironing of his shirt and insisted on pressing his Sunday suit, while Sammy brushed his shoes until they were like black mirrors. He had already been down the road to the public baths.

"One of these days," he told Ruth for the hundredth time, "we're going to have a house with a bathroom. It's terrible that people are expected to live in houses without bathrooms. What do they think we are—animals? They've a damned cheek, haven't they?"

She brushed him down as if she were caressing him. "Yes, love."

"They expect us to live in hovels and pay ridiculous rents for the privilege, work long hours for a mere pittance, never raise a voice in protest, and jump to their command when they want us to put on a uniform and fight for our country. *Our country!* What bit of country do *we* own?"

"All these dukes and lords," she tutted.

"Yes, they're the ones who live off the fat of the land. Let them fight for it. You know what the Duke of Wellington called his men—the scum of the earth."

She tutted again.

"A right military Charlie! They're all the same. My father used to yell, 'Come on, you scum, pick-em up, left, right, left, right!' Well, I'm not scum!"

"No, you're not."

Ruth pouted her lips and teased his cheek with them.

"I told him. I was only so-high. 'I'm not scum,' I said. I was always stepping out of line. He could never knock me into shape."

Her soft burring voice tried to soothe him.

"You mustn't let him worry you, Sammy."

"Yours not to reason why!" Anger brought a tremor to his voice. "Very convenient, isn't it? No questions asked. Just do as you're told. Well, I won't. Him and his patriotic jargon and heroic battle tales. If you look back on most battles they were a shambles of incompetence, stupidity and sheer lunacy at officer level."

"You mustn't get angry."

"I've a right to be angry."

He tugged at his tie in silence for a minute or two. Then he said, "Did you know they used to hold the tribunals in the Judiciary Buildings? Like criminal cases? The Quakers insisted the tribunals weren't criminal proceedings so they were moved to an ordinary hall."

"Your tie's fine, love."

"I'd better go. Now, don't you get worried or upset, Ruth."

Her fingers caressed his mouth and she moved closer.

"I'm going to be fine," she said. "Don't you worry about me."

At least Britain, unlike its present allies made provisions for conscientious objectors and the treatment of them was, generally speaking, very good: a state of affairs which had had its roots in the revelation of the sufferings of the conscientious objectors in the 1914–18 war, when they had been subject to brutal treatment.

Even now a CO might fall foul of a tribunal or some individual on a tribunal who regarded it as his bounden duty to browbeat the applicants, but on the whole the tribunals were conducted conscientiously and fairly.

A vigilant eye was kept on the proceedings, wherever possible, by a small band of determined MPs, some of whom had themselves been COs in the First World War.

Sammy's tribunal was held in public and consisted of five men—a university professor, a trade union official, a King's counsellor who was Chairman, a lecturer from the Education Department and an ex-sheriff. They made an imposing array up on the platform as if a higher floor level was synonymous with lofty ideals.

The conscientious objectors were allowed into the hall one at a time from a back room and must answer questions sitting with necks craned upwards.

Sammy looked for Ruth as he walked in and was reassured to see her sitting beside John Haddington from the Quaker Meeting House.

Then, on the other side of the hall, he saw his father, crouched forward, palms resting on silver-topped stick, his eyes slicing him.

Sammy's chair made a loud creaking noise.

He prayed for a mind empty of past, divorced from present, a question machine. Question and answer.

"In your statement you say you hold as a principle that war is wrong."

"Yes, sir."

"You don't believe in fighting for freedom, for justice, and for a good and lasting peace?"

"No, sir. History shows that military means never resulted in a good and lasting peace. Victory has always sown the seeds of fresh war because victory breeds among the vanquished a desire for vindication and vengeance and because victory raises fresh rivals."

He fingered his notes as if they were written in Braille and tried not to feel the mockery of his father's eyes upon him.

"In the seventeenth century we broke the power of Spain with the help of the Dutch. Then we fought three wars with the Dutch—we broke their power in alliance with the French. But within a generation we were fighting coalition wars against France. After six of these wars stretching over a century we succeeded in breaking France. But our chief allies, Russia and Prussia, became our dangers in the century that followed—together with France, the country that we had beaten.

"In the Crimean War we sought to cripple Russia's power in alliance with the French. Five years later we were threatened with a French invasion of England."

"What's all this tosh? The French are not the enemy now. You are being asked to fight the Germans."

"If history teaches us anything it is this: after all the suffering and bloodshed, Germany will be our allies again. This is my point. Victory is only an illusion. A pause for changing sides. The germs of war lie with ourselves—not in economics, politics or religion as such."

"Have you no loyalty to your King and country?"

"If you are thinking of the soldiers' dictum—'my country right or wrong'—the answer is no, sir. That kind of so-called loyalty is too often a polite word for what would be more accurately described as—a conspiracy for mutual inefficiency. I'd rather be loyal to the truth."

"What if the Germans come over here? What would you do? Wouldn't you fight them?"

"War is futile. It has never gained anything. I would have nothing to do with military methods."

"What would you do if a German came over here and assaulted your wife?"

"That is a hypothetical question."

"It is not a hypothetical question. It has happened and can happen and will happen. What are you going to do about it?"

His hands were sweating and anger was burning up to his throat like bile.

"It *is* a hypothetical question. You might as well ask what I would do if a member of a Glasgow gang attacked my wife. I would have thought there was much more danger of that happening in the blackout at the moment. Or are all the gangsters already in the army?"

"Don't be impertinent, young man! A bit of army discipline is what you obviously need. Just answer the question!"

Fools! He glared hatred at them. Fools!

"I would do what I could," he said. "I would put myself between my wife and her assailant. I would use sufficient force to deter him but I hope I would not make myself a killer."

"So you are not against force."

"There is a difference between a hypothetical situation of either a German soldier or a Glasgow thug attacking my wife and Haig's blundering massacre of four hundred thousand men at Passchendaele."

"Are you or are you not against force?"

"I am against military methods of trying to solve anything. History clearly shows . . . "

"Never mind about history! We don't want a history lecture from you. Answer the question. Are you or are you not against force?"

"I am against anything military."

"Are you a church-going man?"

"Yes."

"Do you know your Bible?"

"Yes."

"Do you know that your Bible says: 'An eye for an eye and a tooth for a tooth'?"

"Yes, and I know Christ made a point of contradicting that statement." Even if you don't, he added to himself. Out loud he said:

"But I am not objecting on religious grounds."

"You are just against the military."

"I am."

"You wouldn't care if Hitler and the whole German army came over here."

"I am against any army."

"But you don't want to fight?"

"I am fighting now."

"Unsuccessfully. You need more training. The army is best equipped to give you that. Your name shall be removed without qualification from the register of conscientious objectors.

His father caught up with him outside, stalking him stiffly.

"You'll be all right if you get to Maryhill Barracks, son. I've got friends there. I've already had a wee word with Sergeant-Major Spack. He'll soon knock you into shape. We'll make a good soldier of you yet."

"Come on home, love."

Ruth pulled Sammy away and nothing more was said.

He had expected his objection to be dismissed even before John Haddington had warned him. He was well aware that only the religious objectors stood much of a chance. Yet now that it had really happened he was shocked.

As a child standing still in the moving darkness outside the mortuary, his mind had shuddered not only with terror but with hatred and revenge.

One day . . . one day . . .

He had never cried as his brothers had cried when they were children. He had never run away like them when they had grown up.

One day . . . one day . . . he always thought.

Now his father was growing and multiplying like some evil fungus and spreading all over the world. His father and his war games and his map on the wall with all its coloured flags. His father gloating over how many men he had gutted with his bayonet. His father standing angelically to attention at "God Save the King".

His father shot up, a giant filling his mind in the waiting days that followed. Time blurred. The past caught up with the present and quick-marched it into the future.

Left-right, left-right, pick 'em up, pick 'em up. Come on! At the double—you scum of the earth!

The fungus had spread all over him and sucked him in.

"What regiment?" his father asked. *"What regiment?"*

And over and over again his mind ground out the same answer.

"None!"

Chapter Seventeen

Alec was so fed up over the carry-on about Catriona MacNair, that in a reckless moment he volunteered for the Navy.

If he had thought that she could have caused half as much trouble he would have kept well clear of her.

He could still hardly credit that she had had the cheek to come over from Clydend to Springburn, actually seek him out at the pend.

Her arrival had been the second shock that night. The other was Madge's unexpected return from the evacuation.

He had been lolling back with a bottle of beer in his hand, his feet up on the mantelpiece, the wireless blaring, and had not heard the door open and Madge and the family come in.

He had never seen her look so tired and dispirited, and the children were dirty-faced and dazed with fatigue. They all looked as if they would not be able to stand up for one more minute.

He turned off the wireless.

"Madge! What's wrong, hen? What are you doing back?"

"Let me get them to bed first. I'm going to fling them in the way they are. I'm not even going to take their coats off."

She pushed the pram aside and lifted first Maisie, then Hector, Sadie and Agnes, heaved them into the hole-in-the-wall bed and covered them with blankets. The children immediately fell sound asleep.

"My God, Alec, what a day. I didn't even know where

I was. They've hidden the names of every place. You can't tell what station you're at and there's all those posters up: BE LIKE DAD, KEEP MUM and IS YOUR JOURNEY REALLY NECESSARY? That was a laugh!"

She sprawled out on the sofa, her big thighs tightening her skirt and rucking it up.

Looking at her like that, pink suspenders showing and milky skin bulging above the top of her stockings, he was glad she was back.

"Come on, hen, I'll undress you and put you to bed."

"Do you know what my tongue's hanging out for?"

"I know what your tongue's always hanging out for." He laughed. "And you'll get it as soon as we're in bed."

"Alec, for God's sake make us a cup of tea first."

"Anything you say, gorgeous. The kettle's boiling on the hob."

He got up, whistling cheerily.

"It was bad enough here before we started." Madge scratched her breast and made it swing about. "All that noise and crush at the school, then the journey. God, it was awful. But it was worse at the other end. We were all crowded into a hall and this man started to separate us."

"Separate you?" Alec widened his eyes in mock shock. "So that's why you're tired?"

"Och, Alec, don't be filthy."

"Separated you, you said."

"Give us a cup of tea."

"Promise you'll let me separate you and I'll give you one."

She sighed.

"He tried to take the weans away from me."

He had never seen her nearer tears. Hastily he poured a cup of tea and handed it over.

"Who did, hen?"

"This billeting officer man. He said there was too many of us and we couldn't all go to the one place. He was going to separate us, send the weans all to different places. I was only to keep Willy and Fiona."

"They would have been all right. He would have found them good houses."

"They would have cried their eyes out without me and all separated from each other." She took big noisy sups of tea. "God, I'm enjoying this. No, I couldn't let him do it to the poor wee buggers."

At that moment a knock at the door surprised them both.

"I'll go, hen."

He went swaggering, whistling a tune through his teeth. The landing was in complete darkness because of the blackout and he had not lit the gas in the lobby, but there could be no mistaking the small figure, the large eyes, the shimmering hair.

"The wife's back," he hissed desperately. "Hop it!" She just stood there looking stupid.

"Who is it, Alec?" Madge called from the kitchen.

"Beat it!" he whispered.

"Beat it?" Catriona echoed.

She was the stupidest creature alive. He fervently wished he had never set eyes on her.

He was about to shut the door in her face when Madge appeared at his elbow.

"There's a howling gale blowing in here with that door . . ."

She peered through the shadows.

"Is that Catriona MacNair?"

"She's come over to tell me that Ma's not well," said Alec quickly.

"All this way, at this time of night in the blackout?" Madge gasped. "Come away in, hen. There's a cup of tea made."

"She's got to hurry right back, Madge. I'd better go with her."

"Och, don't be daft. She looks frozen. Come in for a minute, hen."

Back in the kitchen Madge poured out another cup and handed it to Catriona before slumping back down on the sofa.

"What's wrong with Ma?"

Catriona gently sipped her tea and stared round the kitchen as if it were about to burst into flames.

Alec wished he could snap his fingers and make her disappear. It was terrible that she should be here taking tea from his wife and only yards away from his children. It was downright indecent.

"There's no need to worry," Catriona quavered, before he had the chance to answer Madge himself. "There's nothing wrong with Mrs Jackson."

"Nothing wrong with Ma?" Madge's tone changed. "Then what have you come for?"

"What she means is . . . , " Alec began, but Catriona's wavering voice horrified him into silence again.

"I came to see Alec."

"Oh, you did?"

Madge rose.

"No, Madge, hen, take it easy," Alec pleaded. "She's so much wee-er than you!"

"I'm sorry." Catriona's cup rocked noisily in its saucer as she replaced it on the table. "I feel so ashamed. I don't know how it happened."

"How what happened?"

If only Madge would stop asking questions! Catriona was obviously a female George Washington. She was going to stand there in front of Madge like a wean who had pinched an apple and confess all. Alec groaned inwardly.

"Drink up your tea, hen," he urged. "It's time you were getting back."

"You keep out of this!" Madge commanded.

"Maybe it was because Melvin's gone." Catriona was wringing her hands now. "Maybe it was because my mother took the children away. I don't know. I'm so sorry, Madge!"

"Sorry for what? What happened?"

"Well, you see, Alec came to the door for pennies for his mother's gas."

Alec lit a cigarette.

"My God!" he said.

"You keep out of this!" Madge repeated, then to the girl, "So?"

"I went in to get my purse and when I turned round he was at my back in the kitchen. And then . . . and then . . ."

"And then?" Madge prompted.

"Well . . . he said . . . ," Catriona's voice faded. "I should be friendly . . . I didn't know, I didn't think he meant . . . "

"Are you trying to tell me that my Alec laid you?"

"Oh, no," Catriona hastily assured her. "We were standing in the cupboard in the hall."

Alec leaned against the mantelpiece to support his brow.

"My God!" he said again.

"I wouldn't have bothered him tonight only I didn't know who to turn to. My mother said the children wouldn't be safe with me at Dessie Street and she took them away."

Catriona's voice suddenly changed to a horrible wail.

"I want my baby back and she won't give him to me."

Alec could not stand it a minute longer. He had been as nice as ninepence to her, chatted her up, made her laugh and gave her a bit of loving when her man was away, and this was all the thanks he got.

"What a bloody cheek!" he gasped. "I've a wife and six weans. I've enough worries without taking on yours."

Unexpectedly Madge rounded on him.

"You're the only bloody worry in this house. My back wasn't turned five minutes and you were sniffing round somebody else."

"No, hen, you've got it all wrong. You know what women are like with me."

"She's only a wee lassie!" Madge suddenly let out a broken-hearted roar. "And she's worried about her weans!"

Her big fist shot out, cracked his chin up, and bounced his head back against the mantelpiece.

He slithered bumpily down into sickly blackness and the next thing he remembered was coming to with a bit of rag rug stuck up his nose. He sneezed and howled with pain.

The light was out but the fire red-shivered the kitchen.

Maisie was making little puttering noises in the hole-in-wall bed and Hector, who needed his tonsils out, was snoring lustily.

Alec pulled himself up with the help of a chair, rubbing and working his chin about.

His bottle of beer still lay on the table and he took a swig, but it was warm and flat.

He undressed in front of the fire, not feeling in the mood to strip off in the freezing room. Once naked he heated his palms and rubbed them together, bracing himself for a quick sprint through and a jump into bed.

The blackout curtains hadn't been drawn and the front room was moon-filled with dancing grey dust.

He froze in mid-leap.

The bed was full, too.

Catriona was facing the wall, handless in one of Madge's long-sleeved nighties, her hair spread out like a silver shawl.

Madge was a protective mountain beside her, one freckled arm over the top of Catriona, cuddling her in sleep.

He had no alternative but to race back to the kitchen fire again. He put his clothes on, cursing fluently, then took one of the children's blankets, rolled himself in it and settled down on the jaggy sofa.

It was one of the worst nights of his life and he awoke to find life no better.

His big, cheery, always the same, happy-go-lucky Madge had changed.

She still marched about gaily making the breakfast and

talking to the children and to Catriona but as soon as she turned her attention or her voice on him the good cheer hardened into cold steel.

Catriona was busily washing the children and brushing their hair.

He could have strangled her.

What right had she to come into his house and cause trouble between him and his wife?

Madge and she were as thick as thieves. Like long-lost sisters. Madge had even promised to go to Farmbank to rescue Catriona's weans. It wasn't fair. Why should Madge act like this?

He would have liked to remind her that he worked hard to keep a roof over her head and clothes on her back.

Instead he braved the icicles to give her a cuddle.

"How's my gorgeous hunk of woman this morning?"

"Get off!"

The words had been uttered many times before but never with the contempt they had now.

He felt genuinely worried but at the same time certain that Madge would eventually forgive and forget. He knew old Madge.

There were times later when he thought she had forgotten. Busy times alone together in bed. Or if they had friends in for a game of cards or if they were out visiting with the children she talked and laughed like her old self.

Yet she was not her old self. Quarrels kept flaring unexpectedly over silly, unimportant things and each time before he knew what had happened, she had dragged Catriona up, then resurrected every other female he had ever known.

As if things weren't bad enough already, Catriona became pregnant.

He never could get over how such a harmless-looking creature was able to cause so much stir and trouble. He used to tell Madge he did not like using French letters because it spoiled making love: it was like eating toffee with the paper on.

Now every time he thought of Catriona he wished he had used half-a-dozen. The way Madge talked (and talked and talked) anyone would think he had planted a time bomb inside the girl.

The baby could be her husband's, for all they knew. He wasn't that long away.

Madge wouldn't hear of that, though.

"Oh, I know you. It'll be yours, all right."

As if fathering a child had suddenly become a sin, and no other man would sink so low.

Alec began to feel restless, hemmed in, thoroughly fed-up with it all, and on a sudden impulse one day he joined the Navy.

So far he didn't regret it. He was a good mixer, cheerful, friendly and adaptable. In no time he was one of the lads, talking about "the deck", "the galley", "skiving", and rolling cigarettes out of "tickler" tobacco from an old tin. His cap tipped over his brow, his bell-bottoms flapping, he whistled along with his Glasgow swagger and his sailor's roll making him look jauntier and cheerier than ever.

In fact, there was only one thing spoiling a new and hopeful horizon: the war and where it might take him.

Chapter Eighteen

"Put that light out!"

The shout resounded up the close and round the stairs together with the indignant clatter of feet, and the door battered and shook before Catriona had time to get to it.

She screwed up her face, fervently hoping that the children would not be wakened.

"There's a light from your house shining across on the Benlin Yards. You're endangering the whole of Clydend!"

The red-faced special constable could hardly speak, he was puffing so hard for breath.

"Oh, no, you must be making a mistake," Catriona assured him. "I'm very careful about the windows."

This was true. She had big heavy curtains up on all the windows including the bathroom and she had followed the instructions in one of the government pamphlets which advised criss-crossing the glass with brown sticky paper to strengthen it against blast.

The special constable pushed roughly past her into the hall, hesitated for a minute to get his bearings then made a rush at old Duncan MacNair's room.

There were two bedrooms in the house and both faced on to the Main Road. Only the sitting-room had a window looking down on to Dessie Street. The smaller bedroom, which had once been the children's, was now the old man's room, and the children had been moved in with Catriona.

"Look at this!" the constable yelled.

The bedroom window stood bare and uncurtained.

Catriona sighed with exasperation.

"Da, how many times have I to tell you. You'll be the death of us yet."

He was sitting on the edge of the bed in his vest and long-johns, his goatee beard quivering.

"What's the meaning of this?" His high-pitched nasal whine spluttered saliva through the ill-fitting false teeth. "Bursting into my room with your fancy man when I'm getting my clothes off!"

"Da!"

The constable shut the curtains, satisfied himself that the window was thoroughly sealed, then approached with notebook and pen at the ready.

"Your name?"

"Away you go, you scunner. I want to get to my bed."

"Name!"

"Da!" Catriona pleaded. "Answer the man. You've committed an offence. This is a policeman."

"My name's Duncan MacNair," he yelped. "But you're not the police. You're too wee. The police are big fellas."

The special constable, still heaving for breath, straightened in an effort to retrieve both authority and dignity.

"Address?"

"You've just come up the close. Do you not know where you are yourself?"

"I'm warning you, Mr MacNair."

"Da!" Catriona pleaded, "What about the shop if you go to jail? Things are hard enough as it is, without you making them worse."

Old Duncan jerked on his pyjama jacket then began staggering about in a violent fight to get into his trousers.

"It's Number One Dessie Street." Catriona wrung her hands in agitation. "He's just had a wee nightcap of whisky."

"I'm asking him the questions and he's perfectly capable of answering them himself. What's your nationality?"

Tangled in a trouser leg Duncan howled with rage.

"I'm a ruddy German, you silly wee nyuck. Get out of my way!"

In desperation Catriona grabbed the constable's arm and pulled him into the hall, shutting the bedroom door behind her.

"I'm most terribly sorry! I promise it'll never happen again. I'll check the window myself every night. He's getting on in years and he feels the cold and takes a wee dram to heat himself up. He doesn't know what he's saying."

"It had better not happen again."

"No, it won't, I promise."

"It's for your own good. You don't want the place bombed, do you?" He nodded at her swollen belly. "Not when you're like that?"

Her head lowered miserably and she pleated and re-pleated a piece of her smock.

"All right?" he said sternly, his authority fully returned.

She nodded. Then, her head still lowered in shame, she showed him to the door.

After he had gone she tiptoed to her own room to take a peep at the children and make sure that they were still sound asleep.

She was always terrified that Fergus would waken, feel in a bad humour and take it out on Andrew. She had been tempted for the sake of peace of mind, and Andrew's safety, to leave Fergus with her mother, but conscience forced her to take Fergus home with Andrew in case he felt unwanted.

It was thanks to Madge that she succeeded in getting either of the children back.

Madge had gone with her to Farmbank and without wasting a minute in beating about the bush announced to Catriona's mother as they walked into the house:

"Hello there, hen, we've come for the weans."

Then when her mother had rushed to prevent her touching the children Madge's firm big shovel of a hand had clamped over the woman's apron.

"Och, now, you're not going to stop the poor wee

bugger getting her weans." Suddenly her grin appeared. "I don't want to knock your teeth down your throat, hen, but I will!"

The joy of getting the children back was indescribable. Hugging Andrew and kissing his petal-soft face and rubbing Fergus's head against her hip she had tried to stutter out thanks to Madge but had only succeeded in bursting into tears.

She was so glad to get the children home, it was worth suffering her mother's warnings of the retribution that would one day be heaped upon her head. As long as the children were all right, that was all that mattered.

Yet the children's welfare was so bound up with and dependent on her own, she worried in case something might happen to take her away from them.

What if she died in childbirth? The thought haunted her and she tried desperately to look after herself and to be as brave as Madge, who insisted that she too was scared of childbirth but flung back her head and laughed when she said it as if it were a huge joke.

Try as she would, Catriona could not even raise a smile. The best she could do was to keep herself as busy as possible so that she would not have time to think about it all.

She rubbed and scrubbed energetically at the washing-board; she sweated down on her knees, her belly as well as the polishing cloth rubbing the floor. It was important to keep the place looking its best. Melvin had an obsession about polish and the fear kept nagging her that one day he might walk in unexpectedly and see something wrong with the house. She could not imagine her pregnant state angering him half as much or even being noticed before a neglected house.

Lying in bed at night unable to sleep she mulled over everything: the guilt and shame of her pregnancy, the coming agonies of childbirth, what Melvin would do to her when he returned home and found out.

Alec said neither Melvin nor anyone else need ever know.

"Except, of course," Madge said, "the poor wee bugger's sure to be Alec's double."

When Catriona pointed out that Melvin had planned to have no more children Alec said:

"Who doesn't? He can make mistakes the same as anyone else."

Alec and Madge, of course, did not know Melvin. Madge had never set eyes on him and Alec had only seen him once.

There was something different about Melvin. Catriona had never feared any man as she feared him; and terror went far beyond anything physical. Although, as Alec said, the mere sight of Melvin's physique was enough to scare anyone.

"For God's sake, hen, lie till you're blue in the face. That gorilla could murder me," he said.

"Listen to him!" Madge hooted. "And the bugger's at least six feet tall. It would serve him right if Melvin MacNair did murder him!"

She could not be persuaded that this was not really Alec's fault.

"If I had had a stronger character, Madge," Catriona tried to explain. "Or if I had been quicker-witted, or just had more common sense, this would never have happened. Anything that happens to me is my own fault."

"You make me madder than ever at that rotten midden!" stormed Madge. "You're that simple."

"No. No," Catriona protested. "All I'm doing is accepting the responsibility for my own actions."

"You're daft, hen." Madge shook her head. "You shouldn't be walking around loose!" Then turning to Alec. "See, you! You rotten sneaky dirty midden! I'll never forgive you!"

A day or two later Alec took off and joined the Navy.

It was awful how people affected each other's lives. Because Wee Eck had been killed, Melvin had rushed off to fight in the war, and now because of the trouble she had caused in Alec's life, he had suddenly shot off to the Navy.

Catriona hoped that neither Melvin nor Alec would be hurt, and would have prayed for their safety, but she was too afraid to open any communicating link with God, in case by doing so she might somehow be made more easily available to Him and He would bring further sufferings to her or through her to the children.

Often, as her pregnancy dragged wearily on, she longed to pray for herself. She longed to say,

"God, please give me strength. I'm frightened."

But her mind dodged the words behind the rapidly pulled blind of other thoughts.

It was strange how Melvin had had no leave. As far as she could gather he had been sent to France. He had never been much of a letter writer and what letters she had received, hinting that something big was on, had had bits of them cut out by the censor.

Rumour had it that his regiment was in the fighting some-where in France. It did not seem possible, somehow.

The war had not much reality for her. Certainly there was rationing. Some foods were very scarce. Others had disappeared altogether and become only mouth-watering dreams of the past.

Still, Catriona was lucky because of the shop, and some-times she managed to scrape up a little extra for herself and Madge.

The shop was short-handed, since the young women were being conscripted and the older ones were making better money in munitions, but they found a solution to that problem.

Mrs Jackson and Madge between them had been carrying on Alec's insurance book and one of the customers was Ruth Hunter. Her husband, a conscientious objector, had been taken to Maryhill Barracks.

The wife was living alone and needing work, but in loyalty to her husband she did not want to take any kind of war job.

Mrs Jackson had told her about the shop assistants leaving MacNair's to go into munitions and Ruth had come over to see about a job.

The only drawback was the travelling distance in the black-out. Even using the Clydend Ferry did not help much. She would still need to use a bus or tram-car as well.

Tentatively Catriona had suggested to Ruth that they might be good company for each other and said that Ruth was welcome to come and stay with her at Dessie Street for as long as she liked. They were about the same age and both their men were away : it seemed silly for both of them to be lonely.

She had not had much hope that Ruth would consider moving in with a pregnant woman, an old man, and two children, but to her surprise and delight the girl had jumped at the chance.

It turned out that she adored children and she was to move in at the end of the week.

The only worry again was what Melvin would do if she was still living in the house when he came back.

The house was beginning to get—it would seem from Melvin's point of view—cluttered and disorganised.

What had once been a tidy bedroom for them alone had now an extra bed squeezed in for Fergus and also Andrew's cot.

The other bedroom had never been the same since old Duncan moved in with his empty beer bottles and sticky glasses under the bed. Then there were his ashtrays full of pipes and crumbs of dark brown tobacco, spilling into every corner. The tobacco was not only from his own pipe but from the pipe of Angus MacGuffy, the old man next door who was a regular visitor and who, although almost stone deaf, carried on loud and determined conversations with Duncan in between glasses of whisky.

Now Ruth Hunter would be sleeping on the sitting-room bed-settee.

These were some of the changes the war had brought

134

and it was strange to see the close all shored up and the brick baffle walls outside the entrance. Some said the baffle walls were supposed to protect the tenement buildings from the blast of bombs, others insisted they were to stop shrapnel and splinters flying up the closes. The only thing they had done so far was to cause innumerable black eyes, bloody noses and broken bones in the black-out.

The black-out, as far as Glasgow was concerned, had caused the only violence, injuries and deaths. Every night more and more people were being killed. Yet at the same time the darkness of the city seemed to heighten the senses. The apprehensive ear caught sounds ringing louder, tuned into more hollow echoes, as if each street were a tunnel. The eye saw nothing, only blackness, yet the ear became acutely aware of a wireless talking in the tunnel, or the clang of a dustbin lid, or a measured footfall.

There had been a few alerts—the jerky panicking whoo-whoo-whoo of the sirens echoing in her stomach and making Catriona run for the children and take them down to the windowless lobby in the bakehouse where everybody in the building gathered believing it was the safest and certainly the warmest place to be.

But nothing ever happened. The long wail of the All Clear had gone and everyone had thankfully climbed the stairs and disappeared into their own houses.

Catriona could not conceive that anything ever would happen. The war was a nightmare unreality.

The only real things in life, the only things that meant anything to her were the times she had Andrew on her knee sucking his thumb against her breast and Fergus kneeling at her feet his elbows on her lap, cupping his chin, his eyes wide, intent on listening to her telling a bedtime story.

Or when she was down on her knees with them on the floor playing "mummy bears" and seeing their eyes sparkling and their heads flung back with the joy-bells of laughter.

War seemed very far away. Like Melvin.

Chapter Nineteen

While Alec's ship was in dry dock for repairs he managed to get a couple of days' leave.

The first thing he noticed when he reached Springburn was the number of women wearing dungarees, dirty faces and turbans.

On the tram-cars, tough, loud-voiced cursing knots of them leaned forward, calloused hands gripping knees, screeching with laughter at dirty jokes. Lines of them strolled along Springburn Road, dungarees straining and bursting with bouncing footballs. There were no longer any men lounging at the corners, but women again, clusters of them, thumbs hooked in belts, chewing gum or smoking. One woman wolf-whistled him as he passed to turn into Cowlairs Road and another bawled:

"Hey handsome, you can sail me up the river any day!"

Alec made juicy kissing noises with pursed lips before swaggering jauntily across the road, and the women exploded in great yells of pleasure and hilarity.

The pend stank. It had always been a bit smelly, but he never remembered such a sour stench as this.

Face twisting, he screwed his eyes around. The cobbled pend with its brick arch was always dark even in daytime and it took him a minute to discern the two bins at the yard end. Then he remembered that Madge had told him in one of her letters that all the vegetable peelings and waste scraps of food had now to be put into these pig bins. Nothing must be wasted. The corporation collected the bins and sold the contents to farmers for pig food.

Government films were shown in the cinemas urging everyone to be careful not to put in safety pins or anything that might prove too indigestible or dangerous to the pigs.

"To hell with the bloody pigs," Madge had written. "We *eat* all the scraps here. I even grudge the buggers my peelings. The rations are so tight we'll be eating peelings and all soon!"

Alec had managed to cadge some butter from the galley. He had some NAAFI chocolate for the kids and a pair of stockings for Madge and that ought to keep everyone happy.

The yard was cluttered. No room for a dribble at a tin can now.

Back to back with the line of middens stood an ugly brick erection which was supposed to protect all the occupants of the surrounding tenements from blast.

Alec sprinted up the stairs, calling a cheery greeting to Mrs White from next door.

"Hello there, Alec," she called back. "Hey, Madge and the weans are not in."

"Out with her fancy man, eh?" he grinned. "Och, well, that leaves you and me to have a wee bit slap and tickle on our own!"

Folding her arms across her chest she enjoyed a good bouncy laugh.

"My man'll slap and tickle you if you're not careful. I would have watched the weans but I had to go out myself and everyone else is away at their work."

"Any idea where she is, hen?"

"Aye, in the queue round at the coal yard in Atlas Street. It's not so cold now but we need something for the cooking. It's all right for the well-off yins that have cookers."

"Thanks, gorgeous!"

Alec gave her a salute before clattering back down the stairs, across the yard, out through the pend and round the corner on to Springburn Road again. He crossed over and went whistling, rollicking up towards Atlas Street, his round sailor's cap perched well back on his head.

Springburn had changed quite a bit. It did not look so busy. Instead of the usual rush and squash at tram-stops people queued quietly. There were long queues at various shops too, although it was hard to see what they were waiting for. The shop windows were empty. Alec had never seen so many empty windows.

Signs were up at the licensed grocers' saying in big letters—NO WHISKY. He refused to believe them. There was bound to be a wee nip somewhere.

He cut off to the right at Atlas Street and in a matter of minutes was at the coal yard. A long straggly queue of women and children and a few old men had come with prams and boxes on wheels and suitcases and shopping bags and baskets for any kind of fuel they could get.

He saw Madge and the children before they saw him and he felt a pang of disappointment. Madge had been letting herself go. That was the worst thing about marriage and put many a bachelor off taking the plunge. Once a woman captured her man she just let herself go and got steadily worse and worse looking. When they were married Madge had been a fine, big, healthy specimen of a girl with laughing blue eyes and a ready grin. Maybe she had never been a raving beauty; she had too many freckles for that. But she had a fine skin all the same, pearly and soft, and her hair used to have a glossy bounce to it. Her figure had always been buxom but her legs were long and shapely.

What a difference now! Her legs were streaky and dirty-looking with the orange-brown paint the women used now, instead of stockings, and she was wearing the most unglamorous shoes he had ever seen. They had thick wooden soles and as the queue moved up she clumped along like a cart-horse; but the shoes were nothing to the monstrosity she had on her back. Hanging loose and shapeless it completely hid her figure and looked like an old army blanket.

138

"Hello there, gorgeous."

Reaching her he put an arm round her and gave her a hug before lifting and kissing each of the children in turn.

She had the youngest two in the pram and Maisie was sitting in a wooden box on old pramwheels.

Madge's face lit up.

"Alec! Thank God! You can pull the coal home. I didn't know how I was going to manage."

He laughed.

"What a welcome! Here, I like your new coat, hen. A Paris model, is it?"

To his astonishment she took him seriously.

"You really like it, Alec? Is it all right? I made it myself."

"Made it yourself?"

"Yes, out of an old army blanket. It didn't need any clothing coupons."

"Great, hen!" he assured her. "Just great!"

Unzipping his hold-all he produced bars of chocolate and handed them round to a hysterical chorus of delight.

Their turn came, the box was filled with fuel and he towed it towards home, Maisie, Hector, Agnes and Sadie perched on top with black bottoms and chocolate mouths and the old wheels buckling and squeaking. At his side Madge pushed and heaved at the big pram, jostling and bouncing Willie and Fiona so that they kept missing their eager open mouths and spread chocolate all over their faces.

As they hurried towards home, Alec indicated a long line of people.

"What are they queuing for?"

"God knows. You daren't stand for a couple of minutes anywhere now or a queue's likely to form at your back. And see half of these shopkeepers? Talk about Adolf Hitler! I'm telling you we've sprouted a few wee dictators round here."

The pram bumped through the pend and the box on wheels jangled the air with sound, and Alec helped Madge up with the pram, then went back for the box of fuel and children, then he pulled Madge into his arms, and kissed her and fumbled to unbutton the grey blanket-coat. In no time she pushed him away.

"The cheek they give you!" she said.

"Who?"

He couldn't think what she was going on about.

"The shopkeepers, and they don't give you a bag or even a scrap of paper to wrap anything in. I was buying a bit of fish the other day and he slapped it straight into my hand. I thought he was joking but when I asked for paper the cheeky midden shouted, 'Do you not know there's a war on?' That's what they're always saying, 'Don't you lot know there's a war on?' As if we didn't. Another thing they do now is draw you aside as if they're doing you a big favour and whisper out one corner of their mouths that they've had a delivery of something. The last time it happened to me it turned out to be bottles of some horrible smelling cough mixture." She laughed, remembering. "When he said 'bottles' I thought he meant whisky."

He grinned at her.

"What did you say? I bet you soon told him what he could do with it."

"Oh, no!" She was surprised into seriousness. "I bought a couple of bottles. You can't afford to turn anything down nowadays, Alec."

He lit a cigarette, settled down on the sofa and watched her strip off her coat, tuck her hair behind her ears, then kneel down on the rag rug to set and light the fire.

"How are you and Ma managing the book?" he asked.

"Oh, not bad." She laughed. "But, my God, up and down so many stairs is murder on my veins. I do most mornings, as often as Mrs White can look after the weans, and Ma does most afternoons."

"I thought they had nurseries now for the young ones, and what about the others? Aren't they at school?"

"Och, they say it's too dangerous all the weans together

at that school so we all take turn about to have a few of them. A teacher comes here with half a dozen or more once or twice a week."

"The classes are held in houses?"

Madge grinned up at him.

"You know 'Mary down the road'?"

He blew out smoke. "Don't tell me they have a class in her wee single-end and Dougal on constant nightshift?"

"He snores like a pig as well. They shut curtains across the bed but it was no use. They could still hear him snorting and wheezing away. The teacher complained. She said he was putting everybody off. The teachers get awful harassed, poor buggers. But there's times you've just got to laugh."

Chuckling, she rested back on her heels.

He could see she was about to splurge into a series of domestic reminiscences and restlessness needled him.

"Hurry up with the fire, hen," he urged. "This place is as bleak as a dungeon without it."

"Och, I know. I won't be a minute. Then I'll make the tea."

"What have you got, gorgeous? I'm starving!"

She struck a match and watched with pleasure as it crackled the fire into life that warmed and softened the room.

"I've dried egg," she told him, struggling to her feet.

"Dried egg?" he echoed, with visions of himself chewing away like a martyr at yellow cotton wool.

Immediately she bristled like an angry porcupine.

"Oh, maybe your fancy women can do better but we're lucky if we manage to get dried egg here!"

Hastily he spread out his hands.

"Great, hen! Great!"

The more he saw of civvy life, the more he was glad to be in the Navy. At least the food was good and there was plenty of it.

"Where are they sending you?"

Madge's voice was still a bit needly, and she pushed it over her shoulder at him as she washed her hands.

Trust old Madge to put her big foot in it and remind him.

"There's a rumour we're off to France soon. The BEF's in dead trouble."

"The BEF? What's that?"

"The British Expeditionary Force. The Jerry Panzer divisions are beating the hell out of them."

She gave a whoop of derisive laughter.

"God, I hope the poor buggers aren't depending on you to save their bacon."

He laughed along with her and hoped the same thing.

Chapter Twenty

Sammy's father had often gleefully related stories about tough English soldiers who had served all over the world yet who dreaded being posted to Maryhill Barracks. Its prison-like reputation was legend.

Now, bumping along in the army landrover between two soldiers and with the corporal in charge sitting beside the driver, Sammy viewed the approach to the place from the bottom of a deep well of anxiety.

The barracks were enclosed within a high wall constructed in bastion form with a series of projecting angles, and the main gateway had impressive stone piers.

The landrover screeched to a halt inside. A soldier appeared and spoke to the corporal. The gates closed behind them. The landrover jerked into movement again and Sammy's world vanished.

This other world smelled different. The air was a heady mixture of cordite, oil, carbolic, brasso and paint.

Gone was the leisurely rocking of the trams, the pleasant untidiness of people strolling this way and that, stopping to enjoy a talk in straggly groups whenever or wherever the fancy took them. Gone was the interesting undulating broth pot of humanity.

Here life was all mechanised. Men drilled on the parade ground like robots with stiff jerking necks and limbs.

The rhythmic clump of boots grew louder and louder. Someone screamed through a crocodile mouth wide open and high.

"Iya – eft – ick – ar! 'Eft 'ight 'eft 'ight 'eft 'ight 'eft
'ight 'eft 'ight . . . "

A flag crackled in the wind.

The landrover stopped. The car horn gave two rapid
blasts.

"Out!" They scrambled from the vehicle.

"At the double!"

They were outside another gateway now. This one had a
huge iron door with a small wooden window. A soldier
peered from the window before the iron door creaked and
squeaked and clanged open.

They were entering the detention part of the barracks,
high-walled off, separate. Into an office at one side of a small
yard. The corporal gives Sergeant-Major Spack their
papers. The corporal and soldiers go away.

Sergeant-Major Spack bristles short grey hair on head
and lip and has a bouncy enthusiasm.

"Hallo! Hallo! Hallo!" He struts smartly around Sammy
examining him from head to toe. "What have we here?
The black sheep of the Hunter family? Well, lad, no
nonsense here, remember. You're with my bunch now.
The army, lad. Nothing to beat it. We'll soon make a
soldier of you, eh? Eh, Hunter? The guards here will
help keep you right. Good men. From Blackrigs. You know
Blackrigs, Hunter? Eh? Blackrigs?"

He knows Blackrigs.

Other districts like Springburn or Clydend or the Gorbals
were cosy old places compared with Blackrigs housing
scheme. There, new council houses had windows broken
and boarded, doors chopped up for firewood, streets continuously swirling and flapping with old newspapers,
broken beer bottles and other litter, and everywhere buildings, walls, pavements and roads chalked with gang
slogans and obscenities.

There also, insurance men and others who dared go
about their business in the scheme were beaten up and
robbed, and taxi, van and lorry drivers passed rapidly

through with heads down, huddled low over steering wheels to avoid being hit by flying stones or bottles.

"Reeight, Hunter, Reeight, jump to it. Strip off! At the double!"

Sammy glowers defiance.

"You don't know the routine yet. The routine, Hunter. First everybody strips off. Reeight. Reeight! At the double!"

"Why?"

"Why?" Spack looked genuinely astonished. "Why? Nobody asks 'why' in the army!"

"I do."

Spack nods to the soldiers.

"Ree . . . ight!"

He struggles, getting redder and redder in the face with the violence of his exertion. Close-cropped hair bristling close to his eyes. Khaki sandpapering him. The soldiers have numerical advantage and they are older and heavier men. In a matter of minutes he is naked.

"Ree-ight, Hunter!" Spack's voice bellows louder. "You've got three minutes to get across that yard, have a bath, and be back here. Get going. At the double!"

Sammy stares impertinence through grey-green marble stones of eyes until one of the corporals digs him in the ribs with the truncheon he carries.

The air blasts against his skin, darting it with sharp needles of rain. The bath is in an open-sided hut which also houses four wash-hand basins. The water turns his blood to ice. Back across the yard again, still naked.

A heap of clothes lie waiting for him on the floor of Spack's office. Prison clothing of khaki denims and plimsolls. Under the conscientious eyes of the sergeant-major he dresses in silent hatred.

Across the yard. This time into the prison building, ancient black stone with small barred windows like vacant eye-sockets. The iron door of each cell has a spy hole so that the guard can watch every move.

Into a cell where the barber is waiting. The corporal knocks him down on to a chair. The other soldier cuts his hair off. Crops it scalp-close.

He is prodded and pushed along to another cell. Inside there is a locker and a bed. The mattress is rolled up tightly with the blankets folded neatly on top. He puts the small kit he has been issued with on top of the locker and hangs the khaki battle-dress inside. He sinks into the silence.

He sat motionless on the edge of the bed and thought of Ruth.

His main worry was that Spack might not allow him to write to her or receive any of her letters. It was up to him to decide what mail a prisoner should be allowed to receive or send out, and all mail incoming or outgoing was read by him.

The sergeant-major also decided if a prisoner was to be allowed any visitors.

He did not expect that Ruth or anybody else would be allowed to visit him but he did hope for some contact with her, even if it were only an occasional letter.

All that sleepless night he longed for her, imagined her in his arms in the cabinet bed in the kitchen. And how was she going to manage. She had assured him that she would be perfectly all right. She would find a job, she said.

It was terrible to think of her having to go out to work. At home she could suit herself and be her own mistress. She was so proud of her home.

To Ruth, it was probably the same as to most women, home meant many things and was terribly important. Home was the roots of civilised life, home was security, home was the reflection of achievement.

He remembered the fuss Ruth and all the other Springburn women made at Hogmanay. Soon after tea-time on December 31, Springburn quickened with household activity. Women energetically cleaned windows so that the first light of the New Year should not shine through dirty glass.

Flushed faces and flyaway hair told of much scrubbing and polishing and conscientious cleaning of every corner so that they and their homes could start the New Year right.

In the last minutes of the Old Year there would be much scurrying of feet on the tenement staircases as the women, carrying their kitchen ashpans, ran to the dustbins to get rid of the last ashes of the dying year.

Then everything would be ready, the house sparkling, the fire crackling, the bottles and glasses mirrors for dancing light, the plates of sultana cake and cherry cake and black bun and shortbread piled generously high. Everyone waiting, newly washed and brushed and wearing clean clothes.

Springburn hanging breathlessly in unnatural stillness.

From somewhere down by the Clyde, a solitary tentative blast from a ship's siren heralded midnight. From the Springburn Parish Church came the glorious clamour of bells. Springburn exploded in welcome. Countless railway whistles shrieked. Over the hill from the direction of St Rollox came the deep Caley roar. Above it all was the steady crack of the detonators spaced along the rail and being happily exploded by one of the engine crews.

Everyone happy and wishing everyone happiness. Happy camaraderie spilling out of every door.

He awoke to bleak reality.

"At the double! At the double!"

For years he had been sick of the words. "At the double! At the double!" A favourite army phrase and one his father never tired of using.

It was five a.m. and the first duty of every day was to scrub out the cells and then work down the central hall and from there through the various rooms, corridors and offices.

At seven o'clock there was breakfast at a long table in the central hall with the other prisoners, a guard sitting at each end of the table. Other guards strolled around the hall, ever watchful. Talking or smiling were punishable offences so that the meal was a dour and silent one.

Back to the cells again to fold the blankets and roll the mattress, and brasso and blanco all the kit and set them out for inspection. The stupid waste of time, the sheer useless idiocy of polishing the studs on the soles of the boots irked him beyond words.

He knew the army "bull" so well, had been nurtured on it for as far back as he could remember. He had been polishing the soles of boots and washing and whitewashing coal while his contemporaries were out playing football.

> *Yours not to reason why*
> *Yours but to do and die . . .*

He had long ago come to believe that the army, far from being an institution for the defence or preservation of mankind, was in fact the most dangerous, the most destructive force, not only to the body but to the mind of man.

The professional soldier's profession was to kill and he believed that—especially at officer level—they wanted war because peace bored them. They wanted to play their army games, not with little flags but with real people.

He believed the militarist ideal was to drill and regiment, the process of regimentation beginning at school where every independent, individualistic urge could be crushed and disciplined.

Instead of aiming at the development of every faculty to its highest capacity the militant ideal was the creation of efficient machines; not fostering a sense of individual responsibility and a questioning inquisitive intelligence but making a virtue of unreasoning obedience.

The military used harmless-sounding words to mask manoeuvres that meant death, suffering and destruction. They pinned on medals and played brass bands. Statues went up and poppy wreaths were laid. Impressive ceremonies covered multitudes of sins.

He hated the militarist ideal more than anything else in the world.

The kit was perfect, ready and waiting when the adjutant with his entourage of sergeant-major, corporals and guards came in to inspect it.

Without looking at Sammy, the adjutant jerked out his stick and knocked the kit on to the floor.

"Get that kit cleaned properly."

"What's wrong with it?"

The adjutant's eyes flashed round and for a minute he gaped.

They all gaped. Before their faces disappeared behind their military masks again.

All his enemies.

Chapter Twenty-one

The sirens started to scream, breathlessly, jerkily, just as Catriona and Ruth were about to get ready for bed.

"What do you think we should do?"

Ruth came from the sitting-room leisurely brushing her hair, arms reaching up and back, brushing, smoothing, breasts lifting, pushing.

Each siren followed hastily the one before, until it sounded as if the whole of Glasgow was exploding with sirens, each one competing in feverish excitement with the other and every one out of time and tune.

Catriona put a hand to her brow.

"They'll waken the children!"

"It seems a shame to lift them, doesn't it? Nothing's happened so far, has it?"

"I know. They're liable to get their death of cold being lifted from their warm beds and taken down that draughty stair. Still . . . "

Catriona nibbled at her nails, eyes straining with worry. "What if anything did happen? Oh, dear, and there's Da as well."

"You can't make him go downstairs, can you? His safety is his own responsibility, isn't it?"

"Oh, no!" She was shocked. "Melvin would blame me if anything happened. Oh, dear!"

"Something might happen to you if you're not careful, mightn't it?"

"It doesn't matter about me."

She avoided Ruth's eyes, thinking what a good thing it would be if she had a premature birth. Only things never happened the way you wanted them to. It would be just typical if this baby was late.

Ruth raised an eyebrow.

"Doesn't it? What about the baby? And what about Fergus and Andrew if anything happens to you?"

Catriona could have wept.

"Oh, well, I suppose we'd better get started. At least this time the alert went before we were undressed."

The sirens wailed gradually away fainter and fainter until the silence was only broken by people stirring in the building and beginning to make their way down the stairs.

Old Angus MacGuffie from next door who thought everyone was as deaf as himself was protesting loudly to his son Tam, who had run up from the bakehouse to help his father down because neither his wife Nellie, nor his daughter Lizzie could do anything with the old man.

"You're always doing this!" Angus was roaring. "Hauling me out of my bed for no rhyme nor reason!"

"There's a raid on, Paw!" Tam roared back.

"A raincoat on? No I will not put a raincoat on. It's too cold!"

Ruth laughed and tossed back her hair.

"He's started already. Isn't he a scream?"

Catriona rolled her eyes. "Mr MacGuffie and Da are as good as any turn at the Empire. Mr MacGuffie with his bums for bombs, and Da calling them booms. I'd better get the children."

"How about just lifting the pram down? And Fergus's mattress?"

"What a good idea! I could get one of the men to help." Catriona's small face lit up with gratitude. "I'm so glad you're here, Ruth. I don't know what I'd do without you."

She ran and opened the front door.

"Tam!"

"Aye, lass?"

Tam strained a red face upwards, puffing for breath as he struggled to get his father safely down the spiral stairs.

"Could you send Baldy to help us bring the children down? I'll just keep Andy in the pram and maybe he won't even waken."

"Right, lass, just as soon as I get this thrawn old buffer down to the lobby."

Nellie and Lizzie appeared loaded with all their usual accoutrements, cushions, knitting, peppermints, shawls, earplugs, thermos flask, gas masks.

"Hello," Catriona greeted them. "Isn't this a nuisance?"

"I read in the paper they had a terrible time in England last night," Nellie confided. "There was this woman who just went back upstairs for a hanky when the bomb dropped and she was killed and the rest of her family escaped unhurt."

"Poor thing!" Catriona tutted. "Fancy!"

They always discussed the details of other raids and made sympathetic noises in the same way as they enjoyed little gossips about local scandals. The happenings themselves held no deep reality. Reality was the friendly exchange, the neighbourliness, the warmth of shared conversation.

Lizzie limped across the landing and peered close through thick glasses.

"*I'll* take Fergus down. *I'll* see to my wee baby."

Immediately Catriona retreated back into the house, her face stiffening.

"I'm seeing to Fergus, thank you."

She shut the door. Lizzie had taken charge of Fergus when the child's mother died and had never forgiven Catriona for appearing on the scene as Melvin's wife and taking over.

Lizzie had queer ways and Catriona felt sure she had done Fergus nothing but harm.

"Lizzie again?" Ruth queried.

Catriona nodded.

"She gives me the creeps that woman. If I've to go to the lavatory or anywhere else will you watch Fergus for me, Ruth? Don't let that woman near him during the night if I'm not there. She'd waken him up and frighten him. She enjoys frightening the children. It's terrible."

"Don't worry!" Ruth went through to the sitting-room to put her hairbrush away. "I can't stand her either."

"Poor Mrs MacGuffie and Tam." Catriona heaved her heavy belly across the hall towards the bedroom and the children. "They can't have much of a life."

She kept a hold-all packed ready and she checked it as usual to make absolutely sure that everything was all right. Extra clothes for the children, their favourite picture books and toys, a mug and plate and spoon each, ear-plugs, gas masks.

The door-bell went and before she had time to shuffle, flat-footed, wide-legged into the hall, Ruth had answered it and ushered big Baldy Fowler the foreman baker into the house.

Since his wife had been hanged Baldy shared his upstairs flat with Sandy the vanman. Baldy had the build of a huge all-in wrestler and although heavy drinking had taken its toll, nevertheless to bump the pram downstairs with Andrew still sleeping peacefully inside was no bother to him. In a few minutes he was charging like a bull back up the stairs for Fergus.

Catriona noticed how he kept looking at Ruth and how Ruth's dark eyes fluttered coyly up at him.

Ruth worried and perplexed her. Often in the evenings they talked and talked and Ruth told about her husband Sammy and what a good man he was and how much she loved him.

There had been times when she had gone through to the room for something after Ruth had gone to bed and found her weeping for Sammy. Yet there seemed to be something dangerous that switched on inside her every time a man appeared. It was as if men turned a spotlight on her and she immediately began a sensuous performance, each movement a studied provocation.

Fergus had woken up and was getting a "coal-carry" on Baldy's shoulders. The mattress and blankets were under Baldy's arm.

"Come on, hen." He bull-bellowed laughter towards Ruth. "I'll carry you down under the other arm."

They were all out on the landing and Catriona was locking the door. Ruth wriggled and giggled back against her as if for protection.

"You wouldn't dare?" she said in her husky burr that always lilted up to pose provocatively.

Baldy's shovel of a hand shot out, whirled her round and smacked her soundly on the buttocks before grabbing her round the waist and clattering noisily down the stairs with her.

Fergus bounced up and down and laughed and screamed with excitement. Ruth was laughing and squealing and kicking her legs wildly out behind.

"Let me down! Let me down! You're tickling me! Baldy, please! Please?"

"Aye, you've a rare soft belly. Oh—" He suddenly burst into riotous song. "Stop yer ticklin', Jock, stop yer ticklin', Jock, stop yer ticklin', tickalickalickalin', stop yer ticklin', Jock!"

They did not seem to care who heard them.

Feeling strangely depressed, Catriona held on to the banisters and slowly and carefully negotiated her clumsy body down the stairs.

The narrow windowless lobby that separated the bake-house at the back from the shop at the front was packed, but a space was somehow made for her and with much difficulty she managed to ease herself on to the floor. People sat on cushions, backs propped against the walls. The pram and the mattress were in the middle of the floor. Only the two old men, Duncan and Angus, had chairs.

They were talking very loudly on topical subjects like black-outs, rationing and bombs.

None of these things were acceptable to old Angus and he was always saying so in no uncertain terms. Again and again he tottered into shops and bawled for his sweeties and baccy and whatever else he fancied. He was completely deaf to any explanations about rationing.

As for the black-out, his utter disdain of the whole procedure was only matched by that of Duncan who also believed it to be a lot of nonsense.

"I was reading about them insenary bums!" Angus roared at the pitch of his voice.

"Aye." Duncan's high-pitched nasal voice fought to rival his friend in loudness. "You put them kind of booms out with sand!"

"With your hands?" Angus shouted inc"incredouously.

"No, no!" old MacNair yelled, nearly spluttering his false teeth into Angus's ear. "Sand, SAND!" Then a lot quieter. "You're a deaf wee nyaff."

Eventually they both dozed off, gnarled hands clasped on bony laps, mouths loose and drooping, puttering to life only with snorts and snores of long high-pitched whistles.

"Where's Ruth?" Catriona asked Nellie, but before Nellie could answer, Lizzie said:

"Where do you think? Through in some dark filthy corner of the bakehouse with Baldy. It's disgusting!"

"What's disgusting?" Catriona's cheeks burned. "Ruth will be making us a cup of tea, that's all."

"Her man's a conchie, isn't he?" Nellie said.

Catriona nodded.

"He had to go to Maryhill Barracks."

"Och, well, the best of luck to him. How about a song to cheer us all up?"

Immediately someone burst into "Pack up your troubles in your old kit bag" and everyone joined in. Then they had "Roll out the barrel,—we'll have a barrel of fun—"

Fergus lay watching and listening, propping himself up

on his elbows, saucer-eyed at first, then gradually as the night wore on he slithered down with fatigue, while Andrew slept peacefully through all the noise.

"Sit down, Ruth," Catriona pleaded, when Ruth had brought in the tea. "Don't go through there again. There's too many windows. It's too dangerous, and Mrs MacGuffie was telling me about a woman who just ran upstairs for a hanky and was killed."

Ruth curled gracefully down on to a tiny space on the lobby floor like a beautiful sleepy-eyed cat, while Catriona tried to lift her belly over to give her a bit more room.

Someone handed round banana sandwiches made with mashed parsnips and banana essence and everyone began to munch.

Sandy the vanman's mouth undulated like a big rubber band. Then he swallowed and said:

"The raids are more often now. Have you noticed?"

"Aye!" Nellie agreed. "All over the place. Did you read about that woman buried alive for nearly three days?"

They all nodded, settling down to eat their sandwiches and drink their tea and enjoy a good chatter about all the strange things that were happening outside their own safe, cosy little world.

Until the all-clear wailed loud and long and folk suddenly realised how stiff and tired they were. Terrible tangles of legs and arms, and buttocks bumping in the air, and yelps of pain as everyone struggled to their feet, and jostled about, and gathered up blankets, cushions and cups.

"Mummy," Fergus began to wail. "Do I need to go to school today? I'm tired."

Duncan MacNair woke up with a splutter, fumbled for his big red hanky and loudly blew his nose.

"Christ!" His high-pitched whine sounded as if he were about to burst into tears. "I might as well just go through and open the bloody shop now. It's not worthwhile going up the stairs to my bed."

Tam came through from the bakehouse, grabbed his father by the lapels and jiggled him about in his jacket.

"Paw!" He bawled in Angus's ear. "Paw!"

"Eh?" Bloodshot old eyes screwed open indignantly. "What do you think you're doing? Take your hands off my good jacket!"

"Come on, Paw. I'll help you up the stair and you can go right to bed and rest yourself till dinner time."

Tam hauled his father up by his bony elbow.

"Ah could have been in my warm bed all night if you hadn't dragged me down here." He turned, tottering, to old MacNair. "Ah can't see the sense in it, can you, Duncan?"

"No, I can't, Angus," MacNair whined. "They must think we're awful frisky."

"Eh?" roared Angus. "Who had a hauf o' whisky?"

"Awful frisky!" Duncan yelled furiously. Then, clumping away in his too big boots, "Christ, you'd need a bloody horn for that wee nyuck!"

Catriona stood at the door waiting for everyone to leave so that the pram and mattress could be lifted out. It had become quite a habit to stand there, hands clasped over swollen waist, smiling shyly at everyone as they left. As if she had just had a party, and was saying good-bye and hoping that everyone had enjoyed themselves.

And because the bakehouse lobby was a MacNair lobby, and she the hostess, everyone smiled in return, and thanked her, almost as if they had.

Up the stairs with the pram and mattress and the children now. And Baldy laughing and Ruth giggling.

Up the stairs slowly, pulling on the banisters, one foot, one stair at a time. Not sure if the baby is starting or if it is only fatigue that is causing the pain.

She is so tired she does not care if the baby is starting.

Only she wonders—what kind of place is it coming into? And for a terrible minute she stops on the stairs feeling frightened of the world outside over which she has no control. Then she hears Andrew wake up and sob and cry out.

"Mummy, Mummy!"

And she goes on up the stairs, hurrying now, getting breathless but managing to shout.

"It's all right, love. Everything's all right. Mummy's here!"

Chapter Twenty-two

Before he joined the Navy, Alec used to pretend to Madge that he had a hard job fighting women off. In Dover it was literally true. The place was swarming with prostitutes. Some rumour had brought them from all over the country and the faster the police cleared them out, the faster they appeared.

He had seen two real hairies clawing, kicking, twisting and screaming at each other in the middle of the road, completely oblivious of a lorry that had nearly knocked both of them down.

The place was seething with rumours. It was said that labourers were already digging vast communal graves, enough for several hundred people. A sailor was supposed to have brought a revolver and two rounds of ammunition home for his wife. Some women, it was said, were carrying knives and poison capsules. Somebody was already rumoured to have committed suicide.

The British troops in France were getting beaten and this meant that hordes of Germans would be coming over.

Yet nobody, including Alec, really believed a word of it.

They had lived for eight months in the belief that Lord Gort's BEF was invincible. It was not easy to readjust.

Even after Alec was half-way across to France in HMS *Donaldson* he still had no clear idea of the true position.

"Dunkirk?" He deftly rolled tobacco in a cigarette paper. "Never heard of it."

He was lounging over the side talking to one of his mates as the ship churned busily across the Channel.

Suddenly Alec jabbed his cigarette skywards.

"Hey, Jack! Are they . . . ? They are!"

German dive-bombers snarled unexpectedly from a peaceful sky.

Alec beat the other sailor for cover by a full five seconds. Crouched below one of the guns, he felt the ship swerve violently from port to starboard as it tried to dodge the hail of bombs.

The old destroyer creaked and shuddered and jarred but bustled towards its destination, visible now on the horizon in its pall of doom.

Oil refineries, warehouses, quays were a holocaust of fire, and smoke belched upwards and sideways, giant beanstalks spreading into black clouds that extinguished the sun.

Dive-bombers whirled and wheeled and swooped and screamed and fire exploded and water shot high white mountain peaks into the air.

An officer came half crawling along the deck.

"You . . . you and you . . ."

Alec groaned to himself, following as best he could.

He had a sinking feeling he was going to be forced into the thick of things and soon found from a hasty briefing that he and a dozen or so other "volunteers" were to go ashore and reconnoitre the place.

Already they were caught in the middle of the inferno, only one of many ships, large and small, a motley armada jostling for space in a fiery sea.

Above them the sky darkened and became heavy with Stukas. The planes screamed with eerie piercing whistles that Von Richthofen had specially invented to splinter nerves and scatter panic. The Stukas fell from the air, swooping, diving, so low to drop their bombs that pilots' faces could be clearly seen before the planes rapidly swerved, dipped and shot upwards again.

Ships cracked in two like nuts and sank within seconds.

Noise engulfed the world. The pounding howl of the

destroyers' guns, the metallic banging of the Bofors guns, the shriek of bombs, the hysterical stutter of the Vickers guns firing two thousand bullets a minute.

Alec could no longer hear what the officer was nattering on about but he set off in the motor launch with the others, towing one of the empty whalers, and prayed as he had never prayed before in his life that he would get back all in one piece.

Dead men and live men were bobbing about cheek to jowl in the water. Hands were outstretched and mouths open in screams for help that Alec could not hear; but he could see that soldiers were being weighed down and drowned by heavy clothing and equipment. The launch nosed nearer the shore and suddenly troops rushed out at them from all directions.

Now he could hear the screams. The boat rocked with frantic clawing hands while the officer bawled himself hoarse and nobody paid a blind bit of notice.

Like shoals of piranhas, troops swamped the whaler. A major's gun cracked out from the beach and shot a floundering young officer through the head.

Christ! Alec thought. Whose side's he on?

He struggled ashore and stood soaked to the skin beside his mates. They surveyed the scene on the beaches, under aeroplanes endlessly diving like vultures. A vast multitude of battle-fatigued men, shell-shocked men, demoralised men were milling and wandering about. Others had dug themselves into the sand for safety, only to be buried alive by bomb-made avalanches. Some were just stumbling around like bewildered children.

Alec could not help remembering the times he had stood at the corner in Springburn watching men stampeding from the works lusty with good spirits and pride in themselves, confident in their skills and what they could produce and create.

Here, he thought, could be the same men. What a waste!

Different parties of ratings each with an officer in charge were to take over agreed sectors of the beaches and organise the troops in groups of fifty. Later they were to be led to the water's edge and checked for arms. The last order from the Admiralty, according to Alec's officer, had been: "Mind you bring the guns back." But first they had to reconnoitre Dunkirk.

The town of Dunkirk had once been much the same as many another seaside town with its promenade and its three- and four-storey terrace boarding-houses, its hotels, its souvenir shops. Now, as they walked along with broken glass grinding under their feet, Alec saw a toy shop with its front blown away and crowds of wax dolls with pink cheeks and glassy eyes staring out. He saw dead civilians, men, women and children, littered around like pathetic heaps of rags. Soldiers too weighed down and bulky with equipment and long coats and rifles and tin helmets, as if they had sunk exhausted into death.

The place stank of death and smoke and stale beer and putrid horse flesh and rank tobacco, cordite, garlic and rancid oil.

Noise battered continuously at the ear drums. An abandoned ambulance's jammed klaxon vied with the terri- fied screaming of French cavalry horses wheeling and panicking as the guns thundered; and all the time there was the steady chopping and crunching as millions of pounds worth of equipment was destroyed.

Soldiers, some alone, some in menacing-looking bunches, staggered about the streets blind drunk.

From underground cellars of hotels came rabid sounds of intoxication.

Yet, despite the madness of those sounds and the racket of the guns, Alec heard sobbing from one of the buildings.

He went in and rooted about like a blood-hound until he found the child, a girl of about three, cowering behind a chair on which slumped a dead woman.

"Hello there, hen," he greeted her cheerily. But as he

picked her up he inwardly cursed his rotten bad luck. Weans! Even in foreign parts he had to get lumbered with them!

He emerged from the house with the baby hanging from him like a too-tight tie.

The officer, already harassed beyond endurance, glared venomously at him.

"You effing big fool! We've enough on our plates trying to organise the army. We can't cope with civilians as well. Put that kid back where you found her!"

Alec hesitated. He could feel the child's puny arms clinging with desperate defiance round his neck. At the same time he saw in his mind's eye the vast chaotic army surging about the beaches between fountains of sand sucked high in the air by bombs; men who were scrambling into the whalers so fast that the crew could not handle the oars.

The officer repeated himself, adding:

"That's an order, Jackson!"

Alec turned back into the building. "You'll be safer in here, hen," he said.

It was dark and smelled of gas. A rat skittered over some old newspapers. Alec bent down and untangled himself from the child's grasp. Small fingers scraped futilely at his neck in a frantic effort to hang on. Baby round eyes bulged with ageless terror in a face, dirt-streaked and snotty-nosed.

He was suddenly reminded of his own children.

Often they had clung to him snotty-nosed, their dirty faces streaked with tears. Their familiar wail had a startling immediacy.

"Daddae! Daddae!"

His stomach screwed up. He pushed the French child away from him. Incredulity and panic mixed with the horror in her face.

"You'll be all right, hen," he said straightening up. "Your daddy'll come back and get you."

As he walked away she ran after him but fell and cut her knees on some broken glass.

That last glimpse of a baby crying helplessly on the floor of a derelict house in Dunkirk would, he knew, remain with him for the rest of his life.

Christ, he thought, what's happening to the world?

Chapter Twenty-three

Melvin arrived unexpectedly just as she had always feared. Catriona went to answer the door, thinking it was Mrs Jackson from upstairs, and there he was.

"Where's your key?" she asked in surprise.

He had always been so particular about the keys to his door.

"Key?" A strange high-flying laugh careered into song. "Beside the seaside! Beside the sea!"

He pushed past her and she hurried after him with short agitated steps like a little Chinese girl. She was thinking of the newborn baby sleeping in one of the bedrooms. Robert, she had called him, after her father.

"The place looks as if it's never had a lick of polish since I went away," Melvin accused, striding into the kitchen. "My God!"

He came to an abrupt stop and stared around.

"You could stir this place with a stick. And this floor's filthy. Look at my good linoleum. You've been neglecting my house while I've been away. Look at it!"

"Please, Melvin, there's no need to get angry. You always get everything out of all proportion."

"All my life I've worked hard to build a good life and a good home, and be decent and respectable. You're not going to drag me down and make my place like some of the miserable slums around here or in Farmbank."

"You're exaggerating. You always do."

Despite her words, her voice had gone a bit vague. Now

that she got a good look at him in the light she felt frightened for him as well as of him.

His brown hair had darkened to grey. His wiry bush of a moustache now drooped like uneven strands of wool. His eyes were ringed with black and his cheek bones looked higher and more pronounced than before. His shoulders were still enormous yet weight had slipped away from him, shrunk him inside big bones and a hairy skin.

"I'll clean it and polish it myself rather than have it look like this," he vowed. "I used to be able to see my face in that floor. Everybody used to remark on it. This house was like a show place. A place to be proud of."

"I know, Melvin. I'll do it tomorrow. Don't worry. I just haven't had time today. I'm sorry. You should have let me know you were coming. Fancy walking in like that!"

"Well! Now that I've arrived, don't just stand there!"

"Oh, yes, you'll be needing a cup of tea and something to eat."

"Sure. Sure. After!"

"After?"

"Come on. Come on. Get your knickers down!"

"Melvin! Don't be horrible!"

"What do you mean, 'don't be horrible'? You're my wife, aren't you?"

"There's things to talk about."

"After. After."

He moved towards her and she backed hastily away, stumbled and thumped down on to one of the chairs. Immediately his hand shot up her skirt to rub at her with iron fingers.

He looked an ugly stranger and she cringed underneath him and strained to lever his arm away.

His voice lowered with concentration.

"Come on, darlin'. Down on the floor."

"There's other people in the house."

"What do you mean?" He stopped in surprise. "There's people in my house?"

166

"Your father's in one of the bedrooms playing dominoes with old Angus from next door."

"Old Angus? Who the hell's he?"

Taking advantage of his surprise, she tugged her skirts down and twisted them round her legs like a tourniquet.

"Tam's father. And then there's Ruth."

"Ruth?" He jerked to his feet. "Ruth?"

"She sleeps on the bed settee in the sitting-room. But, oh, Melvin, please try to understand." Her voice gained speed. "She's been such a comfort to me while you've been away and you've been away such a long time. She works downstairs, you see. We needed her in the shop. Everyone else went to munitions, you see."

"No, I don't see."

"Well, she couldn't go into munitions."

"Why couldn't she? Has she got a crowd of weans through there messing up my good sitting-room?"

"No, no. She hasn't any family. It's not that. She couldn't go into munitions because her husband's a conscientious objector."

A broken roar exploded from him. "Jumpin' Jesus! I've been fighting all this time in bloody France, and you've been keeping conchies in my house."

"No, no. Not her husband. He's in Maryhill Barracks. Ruth's the only one that's here."

Her heart changed its beat from a rapid pitter-pat to a big, slow, regular drumming.

"And, of course, your new wee son, Robert. I called him Robert after Daddy. Is that all right?"

"Is . . . ? Is . . . ?"

Melvin opened and shut his mouth like a walrus.

"Maybe you'd rather I'd called him Melvin. But Daddy always . . . "

"Shut up! You weren't pregnant when I went away."

"I was! I was!"

She lied so vehemently, so convincingly that she almost believed herself.

"How can you say such a thing? Remember before you went away I wasn't feeling well? Remember that first day you told me you were going to join up. That was the day Fergus bit Andrew and we got such a fright. I was sick that day, remember?"

Melvin's rage was extinguished, leaving his eyes bleak and a nerve flickering around his face as if it were lost.

"Why didn't you write and tell me?"

"I thought you'd enough to worry you. You went straight into the thick of things you said. Anyway, you never wrote much to me after you went overseas."

He gave a bitter laugh.

"No, I didn't get much of a chance for letter writing."

"He's such a good wee boy, Melvin. He never cries and he's no bother at all. He's so like you and he's really terribly clever."

He laughed again but this time he managed to sound pleased.

"Well? Let's see him, then!"

"Oh, yes."

Delight irradiated her features and she went flying to the bedroom, calling excitedly back over her shoulder.

"You'll love him, Melvin. You'll just love him!"

She returned slowly, nursing the baby with great tenderness in her arms.

"Isn't he wonderful?"

Melvin restlessly jingled coins in his pocket and stared at the doll-like infant in the long white gown as if it were about to blow up.

"Everybody says he's like me, do they?"

"Yes, everybody! Can't you see the resemblance yourself?"

He edged a little nearer.

"Three sons now, eh? Some men try their damnedest all their lives and never manage to produce one."

"I know." Gently she kissed the sleeping child's brow. "I feel so lucky."

"Well!" Suddenly he exploded with impatience. "Don't just stand there drooling over him. *I'm* here!"

Still nursing and cuddling the child close to her she went to replace him in his cot. All the time at the back of her mind, terror simmered. Melvin must never, never find out the truth. He had often threatened to take the children away from her and throw her out in the street for far less heinous crimes than adultery. She had no idea of the law but had never needed to look any further than her immediate surroundings in Clydend for examples to illustrate the Scottish tradition that the man was the boss, the proverbial "lord and master", the privileged one, and a woman was merely part of his goods and chattels with which he was perfectly entitled to do whatever he liked.

Back to the kitchen she flew to try to keep Melvin in a good humour and in her rush she crashed the door open, sending it banging noisily against a chair.

Melvin's reaction was unexpected and frightening. He spun round, crying out in rapid staccato bursts, eyes bulging, mouth jerking spasmodically under the grey wool.

"I'm sorry, Melvin. I'm sorry!" She stared at him in distress. "I didn't mean to startle you."

"You fool! You've always been the same. You've always hared about like a hysterical idiot. You've never had any sense."

"What's wrong? You look ill. What have they been doing to you?"

"What do you mean, what have they been doing to me? Nobody does anything to me."

He straightened and squared his shoulders and bulged his arms and tried to perform with all his old panache. And failed.

"I showed them. I showed them what a Jock could do!" His voice deflated. "You didn't sleep with anybody else, did you?"

Impulsively she rushed to him and threw her arms around his neck.

"No, dear, don't be silly. You're just overtired. Fancy thinking a thing like that!"

"I was looking forward to coming home. It was meant to be a surprise. I thought you'd be pleased."

"So I am. I am! You know I am."

"It was a right rammy," he murmured, absently fondling her breasts. "The dirty Huns outnumbered us. We haven't finished with them yet, though. Britain always loses every battle but the last. You like me doing that, don't you?" He chuckled. "You enjoy it. Open your dress and let's see you."

Clutching at the neck of her dress she looked miserably away.

"Oh, Melvin."

"What do you mean, 'Oh, Melvin'?"

"We'll be going to bed soon. I'll be getting undressed when I go through to the bedroom."

"I want you to get undressed now."

"Not here!"

"Here!"

"I was going to make you a cup of tea."

"A good idea." He laughed excitedly. "Parade around. Make the tea in the buff. Come on. Come on!"

Getting a grip of her dress he jerked it down to her waist. He twisted and tugged and wrenched at her clothes until she was naked.

"Right. On you go!"

Her voice reached scream-height without getting any louder.

"Somebody might see me! Ruth! Your father! Old Angus! The children! If somebody sees me, I'll die!"

"Serves you right for having so many folk in my house." In sudden irritation Melvin scratched violently at his moustache. "What's that racket out there now?"

"It's old Angus going away." She grabbed her clothes and clutched them up in front of her. "What if your father decides to come through here?" She began to sob and moan and weep without tears. "Oh, please, Melvin, hold the door, hold the door. Don't let anyone see me. Don't let anyone see me!"

"Da's bawling his head off."

"Old Angus is deaf."

Shaking as if she had malaria Catriona struggled into her torn dress and with clumsy fumbling fingers buttoned it over her nakedness.

"I don't care what he is. That's bloody terrible, shouting and stomping about like that. All it needs now is the conchies to come out and join in the chorus. And I thought I was going to have a bit of peace and quiet in my own house."

"I'm sorry, I'm sorry. Oh, for goodness' sake, let's just go to bed."

"All right," he growled. "But it's a disgrace. I might have known everything would be reduced to pigs and whistles when it was left to you. God knows what else you've been doing behind my back."

"Nothing, nothing. Let's go through."

It was only when she reached the bedroom that she remembered Andrew, who slept in the bed with her now since baby Robert had the cot. Andrew was still a baby himself. His hot pink cheek dented the pillow and his thumb, newly escaped from a moist mouth, lay ready to give comfort.

"I'll lift him out," she whispered shakily. "I'll put him with Robert. He'll be all right at the bottom of the cot."

"He's the conchies' as well I suppose?"

"What?"

Catriona's voice squeaked incredulously and she twisted round with Andrew lolling soft and heavy in her arms.

"His wife's here. Don't tell me he hasn't been here."

"You mean Sammy? I've never set eyes on the man in my life. Melvin, I wish you wouldn't talk like that. It doesn't make sense. You're frightening me."

She arranged Andrew in the cot, making sure that his

limp bandy legs did not spread over and crush Robert's feet.

"You know his name."

"Of course I know his name. I've heard Ruth say it dozens of times."

"Does she know that you know him?"

"I don't know him."

"Has he never been in my house?"

"I've never seen the man I told you. Why are you nagging at me like this?"

"She's in my house."

"Because I know her doesn't mean to say that I know him."

"He's never been in my house?"

"Of course not. But even if he had . . . "

"Has there or has there not been a conchie in my house?"

"Melvin!"

"Has he, or hasn't he?"

Harassment needled her.

"I'm not going to listen to any more of your mad talk."

At that moment, as if to add to her miseries, the sirens sounded and Melvin flung himself on to the floor halfway under the bed.

"What on earth are you doing now?"

He got up slowly, fumblingly, keeping his back towards her.

"I fell, you fool. I tripped and fell. This house is a bloody disgrace. Toys and rubbish lying everywhere."

"For pity's sake, Melvin, I wish you'd just get into bed and try not to worry. Oh, dear, if it's not one thing it's another." She hesitated. "We always go down to the bakehouse lobby during an air-raid but I don't think we'll bother tonight. I'm tired as well. Anyway, nothing ever happens here. Although this is supposed to be a bull's-eye area and they're so fussy about the black-out. There's always wardens or police or somebody shouting 'Put that light out!' You can't even shine a torch around here. It's impossible to see where you're going. It's really dangerous."

"Dangerous." He laughed bitterly. "Dangerous? You don't know what danger is, you fool."

"Oh, don't I? You don't know about that baffle wall in front of the close."

"What do you mean, I don't know about the baffle wall? I nearly broke my nose finding out about it on the way in."

"You see! You see! The children are always banging against it and hurting themselves. It's an absolute menace, that thing. I'd better go and tell Ruth that I've decided not to go down. I don't suppose she'll bother going either."

"I'll see about this tomorrow, do you hear me? I'll see about this."

She turned at the door, her face creasing with exasperation.

"See about what?"

"Strangers and conchies in my house."

His eyes bulged red-veined at her in the shadowy light from the bedside lamp.

"You tell that woman I'll be talking to her tomorrow."

She escaped from the room to find Ruth in the hall wearing nothing but a clinging low-cut night-dress. She was stretching slowly, lazily.

"This is getting monotonous, Catriona, isn't it? And exhausting. I feel as if I haven't had a decent sleep for years, don't you?"

"Let's just go back to bed," Catriona suggested. "My husband Melvin's home."

"Is he?"

Ruth awoke with interest.

"Good night, Ruth."

Catriona edged back into the bedroom and closed the door. The bedside lamp had been put out and for a moment she felt alone in the darkness with the thrum-thrum of the planes passing overhead.

She did not usually pay much attention to them. They came with the darkness every night and filled the sky like a pregnancy, a menace she knew was there but just had to live with and accept.

She slipped out of her clothes and groped for her night-dress.

"Maybe they're ours," she said, just to make conversation. "Probably it's the RAF."

"Don't ever mention the bloody RAF to me!" Melvin burst out with unexpected loudness and venom.

Catriona hastily hushed him and scrambled into bed.

"For goodness' sake, what are you shouting like that for? You'll waken the children." Then her own voice rose with surprise. "You've still got your clothes on. Have you a chill or 'flu or something? You're shivering!"

"There's nothing wrong with me. If I want to sleep with my clothes on, I'll sleep with my clothes on."

"Oh, dear, maybe I should get the doctor!"

"Jumpin' Jesus, I'll take them off if it'll please you."

Melvin tugged at his battledress under the blankets, writhing and bumping about.

"There's nothing wrong with me now, I keep telling you."

"Now?" She caught anxiously at the word. "What was wrong with you before?"

"Nothing, you fool! Everybody went to transit camps and rest centres. I was rested and fêted and treated like a lord for God knows how long. I'll soon show you if there's anything wrong with me or not."

He bunched up her night-dress with his big fists and jerked her against him.

She wanted to plead with him to be gentle, because she was still tender from Robert's birth, but she was afraid to remind him of the baby.

She squeezed her hands down to act as a buffer and shut her eyes and tightened her muscles for the terrible invasion of pain.

Instead something small and soft kept bumping futilely against her. Then after a long time, Melvin said:

"I've gone right off you. You're no use. I've gone right off you, do you hear?"

She did not answer and they both lay very still in the darkness and listened to the planes.

Chapter Twenty-four

To learn that Melvin despised her came as no surprise to Catriona. What puzzled her was that he had ever wanted her in the first place.

But her husband's rejection of her brought a shame more acute than she had ever experienced before, and her inability to cope with the changes in his behaviour made her feel insecure and confused.

He nagged at her in unexpected bursts and spasms. At other times he shot out sudden crazy accusations.

He could hardly bear to stay under the same roof as her any more, and for the whole of his leave he padded about, high-shouldered and long-armed like a gorilla behind bars.

The continuous movement of him nearly drove Catriona to distraction. Round and round the house from one room to another he prowled, with a cigarette in one hand and the other hand busy jingling coins in his pocket. He sucked in smoke as if it were nectar and blew it out fast. He tried his pipe now and again but mostly it was a continuous chain of cigarettes.

"There won't be any cigarettes left for the customers if you go on smoking like that," she told him eventually. "They have to take some Pasha in their ration as it is."

"Pasha. My God!" He tossed away a half-smoked cigarette and lit another. "Somebody lit up one of them in the shop the other day. It stank the place to high heavens. What are they made of—camel's shit?"

A couple of times he helped her down to the close with

the pram and then he brightened when Tam and Baldy and Sandy praised "the new addition to the family".

Tam had punched him enthusiastically.

"You're a lucky man, eh? Three braw sons. Are you aiming to build up your own football team, eh?"

Melvin had laughed with pride and pleasure then.

"Aye, my Robert's the best behaved infant in Glasgow. I've three sons to be proud of. They're all grand lads."

But mostly he just laughed with Ruth.

When Catriona introduced him to Ruth, he was obviously impressed, and now in his restlessness to escape from the house he often went down to the bakehouse or the shop and did not come back up again until closing time. Then he and Ruth would return together, their laughter spinning round and round the spiral stairs.

"You said you hated conchies," Catriona reminded him.

"Don't you ever mention that name in my house!"

"Ruth's a conchie."

He guffawed and smacked his knees.

"You're jealous!"

She flushed.

"I'm stating a fact."

"She's a fine-looking woman. That's a fact."

She could not deny this. Ruth oozed beauty. Her black hair and her dark eyes gave her a kind of gypsy magic, and speaking to Melvin about Ruth only seemed to make him worse.

He seemed to take a pride in developing a noisy bantering relationship with the girl and sticking it out in front of Catriona like an impudently cocked thumb.

It cut her out as completely as if Melvin and Ruth were members of a secret society that she was not qualified to join. She kept telling herself that neither of them meant to do this to her and it was only her own distress that isolated her, but it was no use.

In between attending to the children and doing the housework and cooking the meals, she snatched time to brush her hair and tie it up with a ribbon, and powder her face, and dab herself with perfume. It made not the slightest difference, but every time Melvin's eyes lit on Ruth they bulged with delight and back came his old peacock swagger. He puffed out his chest when he spoke to her and every now and again he roared with pleasure at some flattering remark of Ruth's. Ruth was good at the flattery, Catriona noticed.

Indignation mounted with the pain of her wounds until one day when she was alone with Ruth she blurted out:

"Why don't you ever go and visit your husband?"

Ruth's smile vanished as if the words had smacked it from her face. She pouted.

"Do you think I haven't tried? They won't let me, will they?"

"Something must be wrong, Ruth. He's been shut away for such a long time. I heard the other day about a conscientious objector who got out after six months."

"I know. I went to see the Quaker man, John Haddington. Remember I told you about him? He explained to me. He says they must be giving Sammy a whole lot of short sentences one after the other so that he's always under detention. That means jail, doesn't it? I didn't understand all he said. Something about a court martial, I think. He's going to try and see Sammy and he's going to try and make them give Sammy a court martial."

"That doesn't sound very good."

"It doesn't, does it?" Ruth played with a curl of her hair, winding it round and round her finger. "But Mr Haddington seems to think it'll help. Anyway, he's going to see what he can do."

Melvin had gone to the bedroom to put on his slippers and when he returned, sucking energetically at his pipe, the conversation about Sammy was abandoned.

"To hell with this pipe!" he exploded at last. "I've gone off it as well. I'd rather have a Pasha." He ruffled Ruth's hair as he passed. "Did you bring me up more fags?"

178

Ruth arranged her long legs, relaxing back and smiling up at him.

"Did you think I'd forget? They're on the table."

Now for the first time, Catriona wondered if Melvin had told Ruth about "going off" her. Her cheeks burned with shame at the thought and she slipped miserably from the room, longing for a breath of air.

Lizzie opened the door across the landing as Catriona closed hers.

"It's a disgrace. I don't know what the street's coming to!"

"What are you talking about?" Catriona queried sharply.

She had never had much patience for her neighbour's daughter and had long ago discarded any pretence of liking her.

"That conchie's wife. She's got no shame. I knew she was a dirty slut when I saw her carrying on with Baldy. I sized her up right away. And to think a woman like that is under the same roof as my wee Fergie."

"He's not your Fergie now."

"No, and he's not your Melvin either!"

"I didn't come out here to listen to your silly talk, Lizzie."

"Oh, it's not my talk. It's everybody's talk. She can't take her eyes off Melvin. Down in the shop, for everyone to see, they're ogling at each other. It's shameful. And the other night I caught them in the office when I was down looking for Da. Disgusting, it was!"

Catriona whirled round to her own door again. She knew her legs would never carry her downstairs.

"The trouble with you, Lizzie," she said, fumbling with her key, "Is that you've a dirty twisted mind."

Once inside she leaned against the door for support. She could hear Melvin and Ruth laughing in the kitchen.

Suddenly she hated Ruth. If only Melvin had carried out his threat and flung her out. But soon his leave would be over and he would be gone.

"I'll show them yet," he had vowed. "I'll show them!"

Melvin was sitting on the arm of Ruth's chair, turning the pages of a photograph album on her knee; and Ruth was giggling as each page turned as if Melvin were touching her instead of the album.

"You've seen all these photographs before, Ruth," said Catriona.

"Have I?"

"You know you have. I showed them to you weeks ago."

Melvin glowered across the room.

"So what? Why are you talking so nasty all of a sudden? It's my album. She can look at it again if she likes."

She ignored him.

"It's a while since you've taken a look at your nice wee house in Springburn, Ruth," she said.

"It reminds me of Sammy when I go over there."

"But you should keep your husband in mind, surely? I always keep my husband in mind all the time he's away," she said with more emphasis than truth.

Ruth flushed a deep scarlet but her chin tilted up.

"I meant that it made me sad because Sammy's in prison. Anyway, the house is sublet now, isn't it? Have I offended you in any way, Catriona?"

"Oh, no!" Catriona replied, furiously offended.

How dare this stranger, this conchie's wife, how dare she come here and make herself so much at home and behave so disgracefully.

Ruth got up.

"I think I'll go through and write to Mr Haddington again," she said.

"A very good idea," said Catriona, too angry to look at her.

Melvin laughed increduously as Ruth left the kitchen.

"What was all that about?"

For a minute or two she stared at him uncertainly. Then she went over and sat in Ruth's place.

"I've an awful sore head, Melvin," she murmured, like a child, leaning her head down on his knee. "I've a sore back too. I don't feel at all well. I'm so glad you're here."

Melvin laughed again but this time he sounded pleased.

"You want me to make you better, eh?"

"You've always been stronger than me."

"That's true."

"You've always been an unusually strong man."

"I know."

"You still are."

"Of course I am! Why shouldn't I be?"

She waited for his usual display of physical jerks, the wrenching and hunching and twisting and swelling up of every muscle in his body. Instead he placed his fingertips on either side of her temples and lifted her head up.

"Do you feel that?" he said, his stare bulging with excitement. "Do you feel that, eh?"

She eyed him cautiously.

"Yes, dear?"

"That strength, that power sizzling from me through my fingertips into you?"

"Yes, dear."

"Your headache's going away, isn't it? You feel electric shocks sizzling from my fingers into your head, burning the pain away?"

Impulsively, she grabbed him round the waist and hugged him as tightly as she could.

She would order Ruth from the house if necessary. She could not stand her any more. How could she live under the same roof as someone she no longer trusted, someone who had tried to steal her husband away. The wickedness of the woman, after all she had done for her! She had been nothing but generous and kind to Ruth Hunter from the time she had taken her in. Hunter! She was well named. A huntress, that's what she was, a horrible plundering female.

"I could hypnotise you as well."

Melvin's eyes bulged and he waggled his fingers in front of her.

"Pain, pain, go away!"

She was suddenly reminded of a jingle from her childhood.

"Rain, rain, go away!" she sang out merrily. "Please
come back another day!"

"Bend over my knee and I'll massage your back. Where
is it sore?"

Her heart began to palpitate but she did as he suggested.
After a long silence, he said :

"You're enjoying this, aren't you?"

"Let's go to bed, Melvin. Ruth or Da or somebody
might come in."

"It's early yet," Melvin laughed. "Don't rush me."

"No, it's not, Melvin. Come on, dear. Let's go to bed."

"You go through just now then. I'll do some exercises
first. I've been neglecting my physical jerks. It's a mistake
to get lazy like that. Physical jerks is what keeps a man fit."

Worried, she got up.

"You won't stay long, will you?"

"Don't rush me, I said."

Out in the hall she hovered anxiously, her eyes creased,
trying to discern Ruth's door in the darkness, then made her
way reluctantly to bed, her eyes still straining towards the
sitting-room, her feet hesitating as if the floor could no
longer be depended on.

She lay stiffly on her back clutching the bed-clothes up
under her chin, eyes wide, ears alert. Time seemed to stretch
on like a never-ending road and when Melvin did at last
appear, she started nervously.

The yellow saucer of light from the bedside lamp left
the rest of the room in darkness but she could hear his big
noisy gasps for breath. The bed tossed her from side to side
with the weight of him clambering in beside her. Then she
saw his scarlet face and his moustache puffing and flurrying
out in agitation.

"I'll maybe spare you a few minutes." The words
shuddered out from heaving lungs fighting to grab in air.
"We'll see!"

Chapter Twenty-five

Cell 14, the punishment cell, was upstairs. Sammy had come to know it very well. He hung against the wall, his arms stiff above his head, his wrists handcuffed to the bars of the small window.

To be manacled like this was not a punishment created solely for his benefit. Countless soldiers had been handcuffed to these same bars over the years. He wondered what it had done for them. Had it made them into good soldiers?

He would be damned if anything he had experienced so far in Maryhill Barracks would change his mind about being any kind of soldier. He would see the whole army and all their barracks burn in hell first. Everything that had happened had only heaped fuel on his hatred and redoubled his resolve to be as uncooperative as possible.

The punishment had been more commonplace at first, going round the parade ground at the double with full kit, or being on half or quarter rations. Eventually his diet shrank to bread and water alone.

The corporal's truncheon had been used. Long periods of solitary confinement had been tried, too. Now it was the manacles.

He shifted restlessly, changing his position as best as he could. The handcuffs sliced scarlet rings round his wrists. He shifted again, his face contorting with the agony of pulled shoulder muscles and bones hot and dry.

The cell door opened and one of the guards unlocked the

handcuffs. Sammy viewed him with a dislike shared by most of the prisoners.

At first, he remembered, before all his "privileges" were taken away, he and the other prisoners had been allowed an hour from seven to eight o'clock each evening in a special room where they could talk and smoke one cigarette. During that hour there had always been murmurings against certain of the guards.

"A couple of right gets," somebody said. "One dark night, after I'm out of this lot, I'm going to enjoy putting the boot in them!"

"At the double! At the double!"

A truncheon jabbed Sammy back to the present and kept on jabbing until he reached the parade ground.

Time for PT now, and he knew what would happen.

He would refuse, as usual, to obey orders. Nothing, but nothing, was going to make him jump to their tune. The guard would report him to the sergeant-major and he would be summoned to Spack's office.

"You again, Hunter?" the sergeant greeted him. "You're a right one, you are! We can't have any more of this, lad. No more messing about. You're in the army now. It's time the army taught you a lesson."

This cheerful speech bounced off Sammy's stony silence and the sergeant gave a brisk nod to the corporal who hustled Sammy away.

What, he wondered, without much interest, was going to happen next.

He did not care. All he worried about was Ruth. No physical suffering could compare with the mental anguish he felt by being out of touch and not knowing what was happening to his wife.

Perhaps she was ill. Maybe people were victimising her because of him.

His mind was still trying to tune in to distress signals from Ruth when all the cell doors were opened and every-one ordered out into the main hall for tea.

He ate automatically, not knowing or caring what went into his mouth, and when the meal ended he rose with the others to return to his cell.

"Not you, Hunter!"

Still obsessed by thoughts of Ruth he looks round at the corporal.

He keeps on looking.

All the other men disappear. Iron doors clang shut. Keys turn in locks.

Silence.

One of the corporals has black cropped hair and skin of coarse grained leather and is called Morton. The other man's head is khaki and his name is Dalgliesh.

Morton stands legs apart, shoulders hitching, neck stretching forward, hands jerkily beckoning.

"Come on! Come on!"

Sammy stared at him in disgust.

"Away and play soldiers with somebody else. You make me want to puke."

"Frightened, are you, eh? A right cowardly bastard, aren't you?"

Sammy eyes Dalgliesh who is already clomping towards him.

"It takes two of you, doesn't it?"

"We're going to teach you how to fight." Dalgliesh laughs, enjoying himself. "F— conchie bastard!"

Dalgliesh's hands shoot out, smack-grab down on Sammy's shoulders. Before he can burst free Dalgliesh's head cracks like a rock against his nose.

Blood messes across his face and fills his mouth.

He heaves up his arms and breaks the shoulder grip. He aims through flashing coloured lights until a jarring of his wrist gives pleasure. But only for a moment before he doubles up with a scream as a boot digs kidney-deep.

"Give the bastard to me, mate!" Morton rumbles. "Let me have the f— yellow-belly!"

185

Morton's fist catches him under the chin, lifts him straight, reels him back. The floor thumps up.

Dalgliesh gouges a boot full-force into Sammy's groin.

Sammy's scream heightens with rage and he punches with both fists. He feels the rhythmic crunch-crunch of his fists as they keep slamming away at their target until the skin bursts from his knuckles.

Noise from everyone and everywhere and everything joins in. All the prisoners kicking and battering and clanging and banging at cell doors.

The leather face bounces off the table. The table does a noisy somersault and Morton disappears. Fountains of chairs spurt through the air. Dalgliesh grabs one and axes it across Sammy's chest before swinging at him with first one fist then the other, weaving him backwards to the left side, then the right, then to the left again.

"F— conchie bastard."

Sammy hits the wall and bounces back to Dalgliesh and hangs on to him, blood hosing from his mouth over Dalgliesh's shoulder as they struggle.

Morton heaves the table away, staggers up and gets the boot in again. Sammy wrenches Dalgliesh round and the next boot-blow mistakenly finds Dalgliesh's face.

They both come at him now. Morton's fist hits him like an iron hammer and explodes teeth in his face.

He hangs on to Morton until he manages to wrench out his truncheon. The success in getting the truncheon acts like a slug of whisky. He swings about like a madman. The truncheon cracks through the air. Crack—crack—crack.

He cannot stop. He staggers about still wielding the truncheon, slower and slower and slower.

He can no longer see the hall. His spine bumps blindly against cell doors, moves along an iron wall until the wall opens and he is sucked in. He falls backwards like a parachutist tumbling into nothing.

In slow motion he heels over, knees floating up, arm

floating too, gently surging in a patient effort to catch the bed.

The bed is no use. The mattress is doubled up with all the blankets folded neatly on top. Orders are that they should not be touched before eight o'clock.

To hell with army orders. The floating arm claws at the mattress until it is flat and he is stretched over the top of it, blood wetting it, and warming it.

Until a whiplash of icy water hits him and from somewhere he hears the sergeant's voice.

"You vicious bastard! You've nearly killed my men. Good men, Hunter. Worth a score of your kind. We won't forget this. Don't think you'll get away with it. You won't. You've nearly smashed their skulls in, Hunter. Some bloody pacifist!"

The cell door clanged and he was left with pain closing in on him. He struggled to ignore the pain, to concentrate on his mind instead of his body.

"Some bloody pacifist!" The sergeant had accused. What was a pacifist? He knew his dictionary definition off by heart. A pacifist was an adherent to and believer in pacifism. Pacifism was the doctrine, theory, teaching of the necessity for universal or international peace, and the abolition of war as a means of settling disputes; pacifism was systematic opposition to war and militarism.

Yes, he was a pacifist and he would continue to be a pacifist until the day he died.

Being a pacifist did not necessitate having a placid, saintly or unemotional temperament. On the contrary, he believed that in terms of the causes of war, placid unemotional people could be most dangerous.

You had to be emotionally involved. You had to have strong feelings. You had to care and you had to care *enough* and caring enough meant caring *all the time*. It was no use caring too late.

That was the difference in the pacifist. He had to be

emotionally violent in peace-time. Peace was the pacifist's battleground. A pacifist was a peace-time fighter. The victory he fought for was the prevention of war. His was the unglamorous, the unpopular, the never-ending chore of keeping well informed about what was going on in the world and passing on that information to people who did not want to know; reading newspapers and other organs of information with a questioning, suspicious mind. To be particularly sceptical of the leaders of men and every sentence they uttered no matter how cleverly phrased and charmingly delivered. To be courageous enough to swim against the tide, to contradict in public places among strangers, or in private gatherings with friends.

Being a pacifist involved fighting after the First World War was over. It meant arguing about treaties. It meant shouting from the house-tops that a Second World War would grow from the victories of the first and the way in which these victories were used. It meant insisting that the end of the First World War was a *prevention-point* when precautions should have been taken against German grievances, not against German aggression.

It meant protesting about Britain's stand on behalf of dictators in the Spanish Civil War. It meant insisting that here was another *prevention-point*. Here was where Hitler and Franco and Mussolini tested themselves, put the first boot forward, stretched the first muscles and found nothing but encouragement.

Why had the powers of Freedom and Democracy not lined themselves up firmly and politically against the dictators?

Theirs not to reason why? No, theirs to reason why, *all the time!*

Pain intensified, swelled to enormous proportions, became like an iron giant stamping mercilessly all over him.

He vomited teeth and blood over the edge of the bed to the floor.

He would teach his unborn children to question. He

would teach them that in each individual lay the seeds of both love and hatred, peace and war and in every individual conscience lay the responsibility for which of the seeds should flourish.

He tried to move but the iron giant kicked him all over and began to grind him underfoot. He tried to suck in air but a gush of blood choked him.

He thought of Ruth. His mind struggled towards her.

Ruth . . . Don't worry . . . One day . . . One day . . . !

Chapter Twenty-six

"Have I done anything to offend you?"

It was the second time Ruth had asked that and Catriona hated her for putting her in the position of having to deny it. She had no proof that Ruth had any particular designs on Melvin any more than on Baldy or any other man. Ruth offended her just by being Ruth, but she could not tell the girl that. It was not fair. She hated Ruth for making her feel guilty and unfair.

Ruth had no right to like men so much. It just was not decent. Ruth enjoyed men. She viewed them as if they were a box of Turkish Delight that she was aching to get her teeth into.

Did her relationships go further than a giggling, wriggling, teasing manner? Catriona had no idea but she felt she had enough to worry about without somebody like Ruth adding to her difficulties and anxieties. She wished the girl would go. She wished she could tell her to go, but that would mean being left without a shop assistant and she could not cope with the shop herself, with Fergus and the two babies to look after.

She flushed, avoiding Ruth's eyes.

"No, not really," she protested.

But, she added bitterly to herself, you might at least have had the decency to let me say goodbye to my husband by myself.

Melvin's leave had come to an end and he had caught an evening train for the South of England. He would not allow her to see him off at the station.

"You'd be sure to lose yourself or do something stupid trying to get back to Clydend in the black-out," he insisted. "I know you. You'd better stay here."

So they said good-bye at the front door and Ruth stood there saying good-bye too. Right up to the last minute, Ruth and Melvin laughed and joked together. Then Melvin said, "Cheerio, darlin'!"

His words were accompanied by a guffaw of laughter and the delivery of a resounding smack on Ruth's bottom. Catriona's anxious eyes detected the brief second the hand lingered on the flesh, and the eager movement of the flesh quickly pressing itself into the hand.

"Melvin." She pulled his arm away from Ruth. "Promise you'll write and let me know how you are."

"Sure, sure." His lips under his hairy bristle of moustache met hers in a noisy, enthusiastic kiss. Then he said in a sudden change of tone. "You behave yourself, do you hear? And remember, keep my house clean!"

They both stood watching his big khaki shoulders swoop down the stairs. They listened to his army boots clanging and echoing into silence. Then they went back into the house and shut the door.

Ruth said she would make a cup of tea.

"That would be nice," Catriona replied stiffly.

While Ruth was putting the kettle on, she escaped into the bedroom. The children were all sleeping but Fergus was kicking restlessly and making moaning sounds. She straightened his blankets and hushed him and smoothed back his tangled hair.

Andrew was back in her bed tonight and she looked forward to cuddling into his warm pliant body and going to sleep with his small hand clinging to her nighty. The cot containing baby Robert had been put over in the corner at the far end of the room, away from the bed, while Melvin had been at home.

Melvin's moods had seemed so mercurial and unreliable that sometimes she feared for the baby's safety.

She had tried to have as little as possible to do with
Robert or Andrew while Melvin was around so as not to
draw attention to either of them, although to ignore them
for any length of time was an agony.

If Andrew was up and about the house of course, he
refused to be ignored. He kept slipping his hand into
hers and leaning his head against her skirts while he
sucked energetically at the thumb of his other hand. Or, still
thumb-sucking, he would clamber up on to her knee to
settle his cheek against her breast.

Robert could only lie alone in his pram in the close or in
his cot in the room but every time Melvin's back was
turned she hurried anxiously to the pram or cot to whisper
loving reassurances to him. He always rewarded her with
the most beautiful smile in the world.

No one would believe that a baby as young as Robert
could smile. They laughed and pooh-poohed and insisted
it must only be wind. But she just needed to look at the
adoration and trust that made calm pools of Robert's eyes,
and she knew, and felt a thrill, and was grateful.

Now Melvin was away the cot could come back beside
the bed, and she tugged and pushed at it until she had it
tight against the side. It was her idea of perfect bliss to
lie in bed with Andrew cuddled into one side of her and
the cot close to the other so that she could slip her hand
through the bars and gently trace Robert's features with her
fingers; the downy head, the nose that was the tiny centre
of the rounded rose-petal cheeks.

Sometimes, unexpectedly, his eyes would open and such
love and trust would shine out through the darkness at her,
she had to hug up her knees and press her arms against her
breasts to contain the ecstasy. And she would lie staring
into his eyes, drinking in the love and loving back with
desperate gratitude.

The bumping and scraping of the cot wakened him now
but he did not cry.

"It's all right, love," she whispered, smiling down at him.

"Everything's all right. Mummy's here." Then her whisper gently rocked into song.

"I left my baby lying there,
Oh, lying there, oh, lying there,
I left my baby lying there,
When I returned my baby was gone . . . . "

The door-bell rang. She tiptoed from the room and went to answer it.

Madge stood on the doormat looking larger than ever with one of her brood clinging to her hand and hiding her face in her skirt.

"You'll never guess," said Madge. "That big midden of mine is back from France!"

Before she could control it, Catriona's face lit up.

"Alec is back?"

"What are you looking so pleased about?"

"For you! For you!" Catriona hastened to assure her. "I'm pleased that you got your man back as well. I had Melvin. He's not long away. Aren't you coming in, Madge? Ruth's making a cup of tea."

"Well, just for a couple of minutes."

Madge followed Catriona into the kitchen with her little girl still attached to her skirts and bumping along beside her and behind her like an awkward tail.

"Hello, Ruth," Madge greeted. "How are you doing, hen?"

"Oh, not bad, Madge, except that I'm missing my man, aren't you?"

"Am I hell! The dirty big midden's upstairs just now with the rest of the weans, seeing his Ma."

"Alec is back?" Ruth's face lit up, but Madge did not notice. She was struggling to peel the child off her leg.

"Come on, hen, don't be shy. Say hello to your Aunty Catriona and your Aunty Ruth. He'd lumber me with another wean if I'd let him. I told him to watch it but he just laughed."

"Aren't men awful?" Catriona sympathised. "As if you hadn't enough with six."

"Seven's a lucky number, he says! Not for you, I says, and bounced his head off the wall and knocked him unconscious!"

Ruth started to giggle and Catriona squeezed her hands over her mouth in an effort to suppress her mirth.

Suddenly Madge exploded in big-mouthed big-toothed hilarity.

"Served him right, the dirty midden, eh?" She accepted the cup of tea that Ruth offered. "Ta, hen. No word from your man yet?"

"Mr Haddington's written to our Member of Parliament about him."

Madge sucked in a noisy mouthful of tea.

"Fancy!"

The outside door burst into life with an energetic rat-tat-tat-tat-tat. Tat-tat!

"That'll be that stupid bugger," Madge said after another drink of tea. "Ruth, tell him I'm just coming, hen. Don't let him in."

Catriona had half risen from her chair. She sank down again, eyes following Ruth's back as it disappeared with eager haste from the room.

"Help yourself to something to eat, Madge," she said absently.

"My God, you've got biscuits!"

Even the child cautiously emerged to gaze in awe at the plate.

"Put them in your bag and take them home." Catriona strained her ears to listen to the laughter and the tantalising rise and fall of conversation in the hall. "I've got a few more in the tin."

"Oh, ta." Madge's big, square hand grabbed the biscuits and stuffed them into her bag. Then she took one out again and pushed it towards the child. "Here, hen, get your molars stuck into that." Then she rose. "Well, I'd better be getting back to Springburn. It's time the weans were in bed. Poor Ma! She's always going on about that. Right enough, it's a shame. The poor wee buggers get dog-tired."

"It makes them girny, doesn't it?"

"Mine don't just girn." Madge laughed. "They howl blue murder. That's them started. Would you listen to the racket. My God! All I need now is for this one to join in."

Catriona followed Madge's buxom figure into the hall.

"She's a good wee girl aren't you, pet?"

She patted the child's head. The little girl was still hiding into Madge's skirts but her cheeks now bulged with biscuit.

"Och, aye!" Madge agreed. "Right enough!"

Bedlam reigned on the doorstep. Alec had a sobbing child in each arm and others leaning or hanging on to him in various degrees of heartbroken fatigue.

"Hello there, hen!" he called cheerily over the noise to Catriona. "How are you doing?"

Madge pushed out in front of him.

"Never you mind how she's doing. It's none of your business how she's doing. Come on!"

"I'm coming, gorgeous. I'm all yours!" said Alec, giving Catriona a quick wink before turning away.

She hoped that Ruth would not notice her flushed cheeks or hear the pounding of her heart when she returned to the kitchen.

Dreamily stirring her tea, Ruth murmured half to herself:

"He's awful, isn't he? But you can't help liking him, can you?"

"He's all right, I suppose," Catriona replied casually.

"He's got something, hasn't he?" Ruth's husky voice melted all her words together. "It's not just that he's handsome, is it? There's something likeable about him even though he's awful at the same time, don't you think?"

"Madge can be very violent. She wasn't joking."

"I know. Poor Alec."

"Not just with Alec. She can be violent with women as well."

"Oh?" Ruth fluttered starry lashes and sipped daintily at her tea.

Catriona pressed the point home.

"Yes, I believe Madge is terribly jealous."

"Well, you ought to know!"

Like guns, Catriona's eyes shot up.

"What do you mean?"

"You and Madge are such good friends." Ruth smiled. "Aren't you?"

There was no doubt about it, Catriona decided; Ruth would have to go.

Chapter Twenty-seven

Madge knew he had gone up to the insurance office to see old Torrance earlier in the day so later all he needed to say was :

"Old Torrance was too busy to talk. The place was going like a fair. He's asked me up to his house in Balornock for a drink tonight, though. He's not a bad old stick. You know what he's like, of course. A drink to him means quite a few. Better not wait up for me, gorgeous."

So here he was, with an alibi for tonight, with everything arranged, and actually on his way to Ruth. He had never felt so excited in years. He could hardly credit his good fortune.

He had tried to talk to her at the door of Catriona's place that other night but didn't get a chance for the weans and eventually he had burst out more as a joke than anything else :

"My God, what a life! It's not worth living any more. I wish I could get you on my own the way I used to."

To his astonishment Ruth replied with a sigh, "You're right, Alec, but my house is sublet just now, didn't you know? There was no use it lying empty, was there? This way I can make a few shillings extra, can't I? Then, of course, it's being kept fired, and it's being taken care of, isn't it? But we could meet somewhere else, couldn't we?"

"How about the Ritzy?" He snatched at the first thing that came into his head. He had noticed the local cinema's advert only a few minutes earlier in his mother's place upstairs.

She nodded, brightening.

"We can talk about old times."

"Yeah!" he agreed enthusiastically.

The Ritzy had been a good idea. Any place in Springburn or even in the city might have meant bumping into some friend or neighbour who would pass the word on to Madge. Over here at the other end of town in Clydend, Madge knew no one but his mother and Catriona and neither of them would be out after dark. Catriona had to stay in with her weans and his mother took so many tablets now that she was asleep half the time.

The tram stopped quite near the Ritzy and his eager stride had him outside the cinema and up the front steps in a matter of seconds.

She was waiting for him in the foyer, looking more desirable than any woman he had ever seen in his life. He gave her an appreciative wink.

"Hello there, love, you look good enough to eat!"

She smiled.

"Hello, Alec."

He could hardly take his eyes off her as he bought the tickets and gestured to her to precede him up the stairs to the best seats in the house. He did not touch her but made the gesture like a caress and knew by the purr in her eyes that she understood.

The film had already started when they reached the dark darkness of the gallery. They found two seats in the back row, and took their time settling down. Slouching back, Alec arranged his long legs as comfortably as he could in the small space available. Ruth relaxed and crossed her shapely legs, resting her elbows on the arms of her seat while she slowly eased off her gloves, one finger at a time like a strip-tease artist.

It was better entertainment than what was going on on the screen, but Alec forced his gaze if not his attention away from her. He was still making love to her. By stretching out the suspense, by not watching her, he was intensifying her eagerness to be watched. Making love was an art, and one he believed he had a particular talent for.

This time he had everything carefully thought out. They were going to enjoy each other, Ruth and he. This was going to be a night to remember.

In a few minutes he would change his position slightly so that he could drape his arm along the back of her seat. She would melt into him, her soft flesh pressing close. His arm would tighten round her shoulder. Her head would move back, face tilting, moist mouth opening with invitation.

But first he would kiss her hair and brow and ears and eyes. And all the time his hands would gently stroke and fondle.

He would make sure, though, that he did not go too far. Even if she begged him, and she probably would, he must not go too far. The back row of the Ritzy's gallery was not for them. Not when there was a perfectly comfortable spare bed in his mother's place in Dessie Street.

He had a key to the house and by the time the show finished and they got back to Dessie Street his mother would have taken her sleeping tablet and be dead to the world in the kitchen bed. Ruth and he would slip quietly into the house, make straight for the bedroom and bolt the door.

He was just about to move towards her when something unexpected caught his attention.

A notice had flashed on the screen:

"An air raid is now in progress. Any patrons wishing to leave should do so now in a quiet and orderly manner."

"Oh, hell!" he protested indignantly.

"Sh . . . sh!" Ruth's eyes glimmered mischievously at him through the darkness. "They often do that, didn't you know?"

Just looking at her made his indignation melt away. He grinned and winked.

"Yeah! Who doesn't!"

She giggled.

"Everything you say sounds awful! You've always been the same, haven't you?"

"You too, hen. You sex maniac you!"

Suddenly the building jerked at its roots with a dull thud. Everyone stood up.

"That was close," Alec said. "Close enough to be the docks!"

The screen went dead.

"Oh, Alec!"

"Come on, hen. I'll take you back home."

People had begun to crush into the passage-ways, but there was no panic. It just looked like the normal nightly crush to get home after the show had finished.

Alec shouldered a path for Ruth and, reaching the emergency exit a few yards from where they had been sitting, turned to allow her to go through the door before him. At the same time his eyes seemed to explode. Everything around him disintegrated in an angry roar. His hands, clutching out for support, caught at the lintel of the exit door and hung on.

Sound crumpled down under a huge puff of dust. Then there was silence.

He heaved himself out through the door and allowed his feet to slowly, carefully descend the stairs.

The emergency exit led to a narrow lane at the side of the cinema. Alec stood staring dazedly towards the Main Road.

There were sounds of running feet in the black-out and weak little fingers of light from torches frantically criss-crossed. People were shouting and an air-raid warden wearing a steel helmet came clattering over the cobblestones of the lane towards him.

"Are you all right? Did anybody else get out this side?"

Alec stared at him.

The warden rushed in through the emergency door, aiming his torch upwards. In a few minutes he came out again.

"We'd better go round to the front." He got a grip of Alec's arm. "This wall doesn't look too safe. You've been lucky, Jack!"

Alec allowed himself to be led on to the Main Road. A pale moon showed the Ritzy lying open at the front like an old dolls' house and full to overflowing with a mountain of rubbish. It spilled out on to the street, with lavatory pans and fancy tiles, broken bricks and slabs at grotesque angles like tombstones in an old graveyard and gold-painted plaster, and great beams of wood, and red plush seats gone grey.

Already people were moving over the mountain, a black swarm of burrowing ants. Others were standing dazedly at the foot as he was standing. Some wept.

One woman was moaning and sobbing and talking to herself.

"We had a fight and he took the wean and went without me. Him and the wean liked them cowboy pictures. I wanted him to mend the pulley. He'd been promising to mend it for ages. Tommy, I says, if you go out tonight again, that's us finished. But him and the wean liked them cowboy pictures, and they went without me."

The air-raid warden asked Alec his name and address, and if he had been with others, and if so, did he see any of them here, and if not, what were their names and addresses?

Alec continued to stare at him until suddenly the warden said:

"Don't worry, Jack. It'll come back to you. You're still shocked. Here, have a cigarette and just stay there until I've time to see to you."

Alec inhaled, his nostrils pinching in with the smoke.

The warden had joined the other ants scrabbling and pulling at the debris.

No one would notice, Alec thought, if he walked away

now. He could walk and walk until he felt better. Then he could jump on a tram-car and go home. He could go home to Madge as if nothing had happened. No one need ever know.

Somebody was repeating angrily, brokenly beside him: "Bloody war! Bloody stupid war!"

He seconded that. War was the stupidest thing that men had ever thought up. Life was short and there were so many better things to do with it. War was a bloody stupid waste!

He saw the warden crushing towards him and tossed away his cigarette. Now was the time to go, the time to say a silent good-bye to Ruth. He cursed himself bitterly because he could not do it.

"Feeling better, Jack?"

"It's Alec. Alec Jackson, Cowlairs Pend, Springburn."

He flung himself down on his knees with the others to claw desperately at the bricks and the wood and the stone . . .

"Somebody belonging to you in there?" the warden sympathised.

"A woman." Dust stung Alec's eyes and cracked his voice. "Ruth Hunter."

Catriona would have fainted when she learned about Ruth but she discovered that fainting was a luxury she could not indulge in. To escape into unconsciousness when two children were clinging to one's skirts and a baby was gurgling trustfully in one's arms, had to be out of the question. She must force herself to go on dandling baby Robert and telling the other children to behave themselves. She must light the fire and dress Robert and cook breakfast and pick up toys in case the old man tripped over them. There were nappies to be washed and beds to be made and she had to decide what to cook for dinner.

Life went on. Mercilessly. There was no escape. The young girl inside her panicked, flapped futilely against the reality of an ordinary housewife shackled with weans, one wife among millions, having to go on and on struggling with endless responsibilities, disappointments and problems, having to accept the pitiless erosion of age and the irrevocable finality of death.

Having to face guilt, having to look herself in the face.

Poor Ruth, she kept thinking. Oh, my God, poor Ruth!

The funeral had been a nightmare and the Quaker meeting for worship afterwards, in which there had been endless painful time to think, was no better.

This was the first time she had seen Sammy since they took him away and what she saw brought more horror.

His head was shaved to a dark red stubble that laid bare bright scarlet weals. His eyes were inflamed and badly cut. Stitches puckered his skin. His nose was smashed and his face twisted with discoloured swellings.

He sat opposite her in the small room of the Quaker Meeting House, his stocky body rigid, his grey pebble eyes hard.

Long wooden forms were arranged in a square with a small table in the centre. On the table a vase of daffodils made the rays of a wintry sun look faded. The clock on the wall ticked interminably like tiny droplets from a vast sea of silence.

Catriona's gaze wandered over some of the others in the room then she tried to concentrate on the daffodils to keep her mind safely empty. But she kept thinking: Poor Ruth! Oh, my God! Poor Ruth.

She remembered how she had confided in Ruth one night not long before Robert's birth. She burst into tears and confessed to Ruth that she felt frightened to go to bed on her own in case the baby started during the night and she was not able to help herself.

Ruth had immediately flung her arms round her neck, hugged and kissed her and assured her that she would love to look after her and she must never feel lonely or frightened ever again as long as she was with her.

From that night until Robert's birth Ruth had slept with her, cuddled into her back with her arm protectively round her swollen waist. And before saying good night every night she would ask in that lilting voice of hers:

"You're all right now, aren't you? You'll tell me if you need anything else, won't you?"

She remembered the luxury of cups of tea in bed in the morning brought by Ruth before she went down to her day's work in the shop. She remembered a thousand little kindnesses eagerly, lovingly, generously given.

In an agony of remorse she recalled her jealousy of Ruth, her coldness to the girl and her eventual wish to get rid of her.

If only . . . If only . . . The words prefaced a dozen thoughts as she sat in the Quaker silence opposite Sammy.

John Haddington, who had finally managed to get Sammy out of Maryhill Barracks, had wanted to take him home with him but Sammy had come to Dessie Street because Ruth's belongings were there.

"You can sleep on the bed-settee in the sitting-room," she told him. "You can stay here as long as you like."

She dreaded to think what would happen when Melvin came home again but she would have to face that problem when he arrived. She had no alternative. Life went on. You kept doing what you could in your own way. You made mistakes. You struggled to understand. You failed. You tried again. You took one small step after another. Only kings, politicians and madmen took big steps like war.

You just took one small stumbling step after another because you believed that life was a pattern of small things, a chain in which every tiny link mattered.

She wanted to talk to Sammy on the way back to Dessie Street, to try to explain. She sought to bring words of comfort to her inarticulate tongue but no words came.

And perhaps she had no need to say anything.

In the kitchen, while she was making a cup of tea, Sammy

chatted quite naturally to the children and when Fergus, in an embarrassing burst of honesty said: "What an awful looking face you've got!" Sammy laughed and replied, "I know. Think yourself lucky you haven't got one like it. You're a handsome wee lad!"

He took it in his stride, too, when the old man spoke about Ruth.

"A fine figure of a woman!" Duncan chewed nostalgically on his pipe as he kept repeating in high-pitched aggrieved tones. "A fine figure of a woman. It's terrible. What am I going to do down in that shop without her?"

"Da!"

Catriona tried to silence him with a hiss in her voice and a cup of tea in her hand. But Sammy's gruff voice had assured her,

"There's no need to get upset. It's all right."

Afterwards he had dandled Robert on his knee while she prepared the child's evening bottle.

My God! she thought. Alec's child!

But she smiled and said what a good baby he was and Sammy too admired him.

Madge had agreed that Sammy must never know that Ruth had been with Alec that night, but that was as far as she would go.

"I'll make Alec pay for this," she vowed. "I'll make the dirty rotten midden regret this for the rest of his f— life."

"Madge!"

Catriona had been shocked and distressed, not only by Madge's language but by the ugly bitterness twisting the normally placid, good-natured face.

"Madge, please. What's the good of being like that. You'll only make yourself ill. I'm sure Alec will regret that night without you making his life a misery."

"What do you know about misery?" Madge shouted. "What do you know about anything? Coddled and spoiled and doted on all your life by your 'mummy'."

"Madge, don't."

"Your own man wasn't enough for you. You had to have a taste of mine as well."

"You're upset. I know how you must feel. But hating me won't change Alec."

"You mind you own f— business. You've had more than enough to do with my man. God knows how many other wee cows have had their fun and games with him as well. To think there was a time when I actually trusted him. But never again! He's made a fool of me once too often. Don't you tell me how I should or shouldn't be with him!"

She agreed, however, that no good purpose would be served by allowing Sammy to know.

It was comfort Sammy needed, and that first night in Dessie Street, Catriona's tongue still desperately searched for words: Eventually, before saying good night to him, she managed:

"Ruth used to talk about you all the time, Sammy. She loved you very much and she was always so proud of you."

Was that small step a failure, she wondered, lying in bed across the hall from Sammy, sharing the same darkness and the terrible sound of his sobbing.

She clutched at the bars of the baby's cot, longing to go through and hold the man, and hush and soothe him as she would the baby.

But she remained clutching the bars, imprisoned.

Chapter Twenty-eight

"You're like a hen on a hot girdle," Duncan complained. "You're more of a hindrance than a help in this shop. Ruth took her time but she got things done no bother."

"All right! All right! So I'm not Ruth!" Catriona hissed, turning to the next customer.

Her father-in-law was still muttering and salivating into his goatee beard after all the customers had gone.

"I'll leave you to lock up, Da," she told him. "I'll have to hurry upstairs."

"Some employee you make!"

"I'm not an employee."

"Ruth always stayed behind and saw to everything. I never needed to worry."

"Well, *I* need to worry. I've a baby lying in a pram in that draughty close and I've another baby upstairs in Mrs Jackson's and Fergus has been home from school for ages and I dread to think where he is and what he's doing. And I've everybody's tea to see to."

"That conchie nyuck up there should be doing something for his keep. What's he doing, eh?"

"He's paying good money for his keep and he's away seeing about a job today."

"Aye, he'll be getting himself fixed up in one of them boom factories. He'll make his pile here while the likes of Melvin's away earning coppers. I told that stupid ass that I could have got him deferred. He's no right to go away and leave me to look after this business by myself at my age. If the likes of that conchie can stay here and make his pile . . ."

"Oh, for goodness' sake, Da!" she interrupted impatiently. "Sammy would rather die than go into munitions. He's a pacifist. He's gone to see his Quaker friends. They have an ambulance service. They do jobs like that."

"Bloody pacifists! They ought to put them up against a wall and shoot them!"

"Da, you know you don't mean that. You're just tired and needing your tea. I'll away upstairs and get it started."

Unexpectedly the door-bell pinged and a traveller shuffled in with no legs, only feet showing on the end of his long, blue belted raincoat. The coat, shined smooth with age and years of carrying bulky samples, was topped by a milky-moon face devoid of any expression except resignation. His black homburg looked as if somebody had stamped on it and twisted the brim in a fit of rage, a misfortune he had no doubt suffered with the same stoic lack of emotion with which he put up with everything else.

"What have you got?" MacNair eagerly pounced on the traveller before he'd even had time to heave his case up on the counter.

"Bana . . . ."

"Bananas?"

Excitement exploded Catriona and the old man into one voice.

"Banana essence. You can make a spread for sandwiches with it. I've got a recipe in my case somewhere. Parsnips or swedes or something like that you use. If you can get them. You cook them and mash them up with the essence."

Catriona sighed.

"Everybody knows that." She took off her apron. "Fancy my Andrew has never seen a banana in his life. It's hard to imagine that I actually used to eat them and never give them a thought."

"Bananas!" the traveller sighed, remembering. "Marvellous things!"

"Them were the days!" the old man reminisced along with him. "Before all these ration books and coupons.

Christ, you need to be a Philadelphia lawyer to sort everything out now. It's terrible."

The traveller looked around the empty, dusty shelves.

"This place used to be packed. You always carried a good stock."

The old man chewed his loose dentures for a minute before saying dreamily.

"Everything from currant buns to sanitary towels I had in here."

"Now we spend most of our time cutting out bits of paper from ration books." Catriona rolled her eyes heavenwards. "Forms, and ration books and coupons. I know how Da feels."

"Aye, my shop used to be the best stocked shop for miles around, but now look at all I have! A silly wee lump of butter and a wee bag of tea and sugar. That would have been just about enough to feed one family in them days. Now I've to share it out among everybody. Remember my mutton pies and my nice white bread and rolls?"

"My God!" the traveller said.

"Thick and juicy with meat them pies were. And the bread snowy white with a crispy crust on the top."

"Da, don't be cruel. Tormenting folk doesn't help. I'm away upstairs."

Catriona pushed through the piece of sack-cloth that served as a curtain between the shop and the lobby at the back, and went out through the side door into the close.

Despite the hood of the pram being up, and several blankets and covers, a woolly bonnet, coat, leggings and mittens, Robert's face was pale with cold and his nose looked like a maraschino cherry.

"Och, mummy's poor wee love."

Hurriedly Catriona lowered the hood and began to unfasten the waterproof cover.

"I would have had you inside in the lobby but you've got to get some fresh air some time."

His eyes beamed love up at her and his mouth opened the

whole width of his face, and her heart melted towards him as he showed her every part of his toothless pink gums.

"I'll carry the pram up."

Sammy's voice made her swing round. It had a jerky gruffness that always startled her when she was not expecting it. She could never quite get used to his appearance, either. His spiky hair, his broken nose and aggressive stare made him look more like a prize-fighter than anything else.

"Oh, it's you. I didn't expect you back so early."

She lifted the baby and followed Sammy up the stairs.

"I came across in the ferry," he told her. "It saves a bit of time and it's handy being at the end of the street."

"I never use it. I don't like walking down Wine Row."

"Wine Row?"

"The other end of Dessie Street. Everybody calls it Wine Row because of the sheebeens and the meths drinkers.'

"I don't suppose they'd do you any harm. They seem to be away in a world of their own."

"Oh, it's not that I'm frightened. It just makes me feel sad to look at them."

They went into the house and Catriona hurried through to the kitchen to see if the fire was still lit.

Any kind of fuel was desperately difficult to come by and coalmen no longer bothered to deliver what little they had.

You had to go to the coalyards and queue up in the hopes of getting a ration of coke or wood, or now and then some briquettes made from nobody knew what.

Catriona had built the fire up very carefully with wet newspapers, a few briquettes and plenty of dross.

"Oh, good!" she said, seeing the faint red glimmer underneath all the smoky black. "It's still in. Now wee Robert's nose will get a chance to thaw out."

Tenderly she kissed the nose before sitting down, balancing the baby on her knees and stripping off the bonnet, mitts and coat.

Fergus was lying back on the opposite chair reading a book.

"Hello, son," she greeted him. "Are you hungry for your tea?"

"I've been hungry for ages."

"Well, it won't be long now. You start setting the table and maybe Uncle Sammy will run up to Mrs Jackson's for Andrew."

"Right," Sammy agreed. "I'll go and fetch him now."

Fergus carefully put a marker in his book before laying it down and it was a minute or two before a question registered in Catriona's mind.

"What was that you put in your book, Fergus?"

"It's to mark my place."

"I know. But what is it? Let me see."

It was a letter from Melvin.

"When did this arrive? How did you get it? You're a very bad boy, Fergus. You must never touch other people's letters."

"It was Andrew," Fergus said. "Andrew gave it to me."

Catriona sighed.

"Oh, Fergus, for goodness' sake go and set the table."

She propped the happy, gurgling baby against the cushion behind her and hastily ripped open the letter.

One minute later she had torn the envelope and its contents into shreds and was about to poke them into the fire when she realised that one jab at the carefully balanced dross might collapse the whole thing in a belch of black smoke and completely extinguish the tiny red promise of heat.

She put the poker down and stuffed the paper into the pocket of her dress instead.

Lizzie must have written to Melvin and told him about Sammy staying in the house.

"By the time you get this letter", he wrote, "I'll be overseas again and what have I got to think of when I'm away? I'll think up ways of doing that conchie. I'll practise my physical jerks night and day, especially my hand grips. Even under my blankets at night I'll do my hand grips. Because the first thing I'm going to do when I meet that conchie is to take him unawares and shake him by the hand. 'Hello there,' I'll say in a big friendly voice while I'm crushing his hand to pulp and splinters."

Sometimes she suspected that Melvin was a little mad, and now she feared that the madness of war might combine with his own madness and swell it to dangerous proportions.

She looked ahead to the time when Melvin would return, and a wave of apprehension threatened to swamp her. Then Andrew's plump little figure appeared at her elbow and she had to hold back the wave. She had to smile lovingly down at him.

"Are you a hungry wee boy too, eh?"

It was a blessing, she told herself, that she had plenty to do to keep herself occupied. She was almost glad now that she had to help in the shop. To keep busy with a host of little tasks and duties was essential. This was the lifeline to which she must cling. The little things were the most important. The tin of beans she was busily opening at this moment to feed her children with. The pot on the cooker to heat them. The spoons the children were clutching in eager anticipation.

All the little necessities of normal life. The washing-up cloth. The plug for the sink. The baby's bottle, bouncy brown teats. His bath in front of the fire. The cracked yellow duck that swam lopsided.

The chipped cup that she kept for herself. The extra cup of tea in the teapot to be drunk after all the children were attended to. Teddy bears and golliwogs and comforters. All the bits and pieces that were needed in life and were part of the pattern.

"You look tired."

Sammy flashed her a look from under jutting brows.

The kitchen was cleared, the children asleep, and the

old man was listening to his wireless and enjoying a pipe through in his own room.

Catriona nodded. She was thinking that it was time for air-raid warning to go, and her eyes strayed up to the clock as the sirens began to wail.

She felt so tired, she would have liked to close her eyes and drop off to sleep right there and then on the chair.

No hope of that, though. There was not much chance of a sleep anywhere now. She might as well get ready for the trek downstairs.

The nightly racket had become earsplitting, the painful din of giant fireworks exploding and vibrating all the time in the echo chamber of the head.

"Nothing to worry about," people assured each other. "It's only our own guns."

The big guns on the ships and the guns on the docks. And all the ack-ack guns firing from the street.

As Sammy carried Fergus and the mattress downstairs to the bakehouse lobby and then Robert in his pram and then Andrew, Catriona struggled to concentrate on gathering together all the bits and pieces and odds and ends, trying not to be engulfed or confused by the appalling din, the hysterical wailing of sirens, the low thrum of planes sounding too heavy for the roof to hold, the sharp crack-crack so near that it violently rattled the windows, the (so-far) distant crump-crump of bombs.

They greeted each other cheerily in the bakehouse lobby, shouting at the pitch of their voices to make themselves heard above the pandemonium outside.

"Hello, Nellie! Is your stomach still bad, hen? I've brought a wee pinch of baking soda just in case."

"Oh, ta! You could have had a spoonful of my sugar if it hadn't been for Paw. I was saving it in a jar," Nellie wailed. "Paw thought it was washing soda and emptied it into a basin of hot water and steeped his feet in it."

"Oh, my God!"

There was a howl of sympathy.

Angus's son Tam, the wee white-haired baker with the big muscly arms, came barging through with two chairs above his head.

"Here's your seat, Paw, and yours, Mr MacNair."

The old men's chairs were always placed as near as possible to the lavatory door. Robert's pram and the mattress with Fergus and Andrew were set in the middle. Then with much squeezing and pushing and grunting everyone settled down, their backs supported by pillows, cushions and lobby walls, arms and legs tangled together.

"Watch my feet, for pity's sake," Sandy the vanman pleaded. "See, if anybody tramps on my bunions . . . !"

His floppy bloodhound face screwed up at the thought.

"Look at that wee pet." Catriona nodded towards the baby. "Wide awake and not a whimper."

She was sitting on the floor at the side of the pram with her knees hugged up under her chin. Leaning her head to one side she began to sing to the baby, who stared at her wide-eyed with delight.

"Wee Willie Winkie,
Runs through the town,
Up stairs and down stairs
In his night-gown,
Tirling at the window,
Crying at the lock,—
Are all the weans in their beds,
For it's now ten o'clock?"

Baldy Fowler appeared, huge and merry and slightly drunk, staggered over everybody and made a place for himself.

"Come on! Come on!" he hollered. "The crowd of you aren't cheery enough tonight, where's all the Glasgow spirit gone?"

"Down your throat!" somebody replied and sent up a roar of laughter.

"Let's have a song." Baldy waved a fist about as if he had a flag in it. "Let's have a good old Glasgow song!"

"Right!" Tam smacked his palms together and gave them an energetic rub. "Here we go, then. Everybody together:

"I belong to Glasgow!
Dear old Glasgow Town—
But—there's something the matter with Glasgow for—
It's going round and round!
I'm only a common old working chap—as anyone here
    can see—
But—when I get a couple of drinks on a Saturday—
Glasgow belongs to me!"

After several repeats, delivered with great gusto, it was decided that it was time for Catriona to make tea.

She smiled to herself as she set the cups out on a tray.

They were belting out another one now, their broad voices energetically bouncing and swaggering with typical Glasgow panache.

"Just a wee doch and doris,
Just a wee yin that's a',
Just a wee doch and doris,
Before ye gang awa',
There's a wee wifie waitin'
In a wee but and ben,
And if you say 'it's a braw bricht moonlicht nicht',
Yer aw richt, ye ken!"

The song screeched to an end in a howling bedlam of laughter, above and outside of which Catriona distinguished a fast, piercing whistle.

Then the building collapsed.

For a few minutes the protesting roar of the tenement took possession of Catriona's brain. She was deafened, blinded, knocked off balance. She found herself on her hands and knees wandering around in circles like a bewildered animal. The air parched and thickened with plaster dust. Her eyes stung. She began to cough.

Then other sounds filtered through the blackness. Moans, and muffled bursts of screaming punctuated by brief disbelieving silences. There was sifting, sighing sounds, and creaking, splintering sounds. The old building groaned as it disintegrated, with as much anguish as the people who were part of it.

A high, reedy voice squealed:

"Mummy! Mummy! Mummy!"

It stabbed Catriona to life, made her claw like a maniac towards it, ignoring the jagged stones and twisted metal tearing at her body.

"It's all right, wee lovey. It's all right, Mummy's here!"

She reached Andy's legs and wrenched up the piece of wood that covered the rest of him.

"You're all right, Andy. You're all right, son. You're all right."

Blindly she fought to pull him into her arms.

"Mummy's going to make everything all right. Mummy won't let anything hurt you."

Mummy won't let anything hurt you. Who took this right away from me? she thought.

She waited for endless time, hushing and holding the child in her arms, waited and listened to the moans and the screams and the sounds of people far off. Until at last hands came towards her and lifted her with the child out of the tomb into a dark winter's morning.

An army of black ghosts was wandering across the Main Road towards the ferry.

Dazedly, with Andrew cradled in her arms, Catriona joined them.

There was nowhere else to go. All round her Clydend was burning.

Chapter Twenty-nine

Across at the other side of the river people were gathering to watch helplessly as Clydend went up in flames, a red ball in a black sky.

When it was realised that their side of the river might soon be an inferno it was decided to get survivors shuttled as far away as possible from the docks and the built-up working-class area, away to the wealthy country districts of Bearsden and Milngavie.

Already, as if the thought had flown around the inhabitants by telepathy, motor cars were rolling in to block the streets by the riverside, queuing nose to tail. Hands gripping steering-wheels, eyes straining to peer through windscreens, their drivers waited impatiently as the Clydend ferry slid towards them, emerging slowly and smoothly from the flames over the black mirror of water. The Clyde was a-riot with leaping, glowing reflection as if a red-hot sunrise had exploded across it.

As the ferry drew in and the heavy chains clanked, the drivers contracted stomach muscles, clutched steering-wheels tighter and braced themselves for the hysterical invasion of the hurt and the distraught.

Instead, the ferry brought only a strange immobility, and utter silence. The whole thing was uncanny. The people of Clydend stood packed together yet completely alone, every soul suspended in silence behind a vacant mask.

For a minute or two, the watchers fell into the same immobility. Then suddenly movement scattered everything in a flurry and rush.

People squeezed on to the ferry, took the Clydend folk by the arms and led them off in a buzz of activity and strange posh accents.

Somebody put Catriona into the back seat of a car and she sat automatically nursing Andrew in her arms and staring straight ahead. She had never been in a private motor car in her life. She just could not be in one now. It was a fragment of a dream. A dream that she was a part of, though as in all dreams she was watching it from somewhere outside. All she needed to do was to be patient. Sooner or later dreams, even nightmares, came to an end.

The car sped on and by the time hands helped her out darkness was beginning to fade into misty grey light.

Somebody said:

"You're all right now. Don't worry, nothing ever happens here. This is Bearsden!"

The air reeked with burnt porridge.

Another voice:

"The ladies are making breakfast for all of you in the church hall."

"I want my baby," Catriona said.

"You've got your baby in your arms, dear. George, I suppose I ought to take the child from her. Under all that dirt he might be injured. Oh, my God!"

A woman's face came nearer. The face was delicately painted and topped by a glossy fur hat. The hat was knocked sideways in the woman's struggle to wrench Andrew away.

Andrew was gone.

People milled about. The porridge smell grew stonger. Faces blurred in a confusion of movement and an excited babble. Expensively dressed women fluttered about near to tears and waving spoons. Voices swooped into a circle of echoes and spun around.

"My baby! My baby!"

"Yes, yes," somebody gasped with harassment. "Lots of families have become separated. There's children all over

218

the place. We're trying our best to get everybody organised."

Over at the other end of the hall she saw Fergus, listening intently to a man who was hunkered down in front of him holding his hands.

She thought she saw Sammy.

"I want my baby!"

"There's lots of places he could be," a kindlier tone assured her. "They've taken children to Milngavie as well. Try not to worry. You'll find him."

She wandered away from the hall and discovered the road outside busy with movement. A stream of cars was shuttling to and from the river. In comparison, the pavement was quiet and cool. It glimmered with early morning dew like a carpet of stars. The stars winked at her, here, there, everywhere, minute yet diamond-clear, flashing up in vivid sparkle, disappearing, darting, dazzling.

She had been walking for a minute or two before she became aware of a car slowing alongside her. The driver, a young man with an eager to please face, was asking her if she wanted a lift. She got into the car without saying anything and the young man eyed her uncertainly and asked.

"Are you all right? Are you sure you know what you're doing?"

She knew what she was doing, all right. She was going back for Robert.

It was daylight now and the fires of Clydend had been extinguished. Most of the district was a heap of rubble but miraculously some tenement buildings or parts of buildings were left standing. Some people had returned to, or perhaps had never left, those houses that had escaped serious damage.

Ambulances were trying to manoeuvre through blocked streets. Air-raid wardens and police in steel helmets and men in shirt sleeves and women with dirt-streaked faces were digging in the grey mountains of rubble.

Catriona went to the heap of stones and debris that once had been Number One Dessie Street. Her feet stumbled over it until she was picking her way cautiously on all fours. She stopped at what she thought might be the right part. Maybe under here was some remnant that would prove to her that she was home.

She began lifting stones and chunks of rubble and setting them neatly aside.

She found a red velvet cushion and a pudding spoon, a rubber hot-water bottle and a knitted woollen rabbit.

Important things.

She concentrated on her digging with great care and attention.

But from somewhere a wireless was harassing the air with unnecessary sound.

" . . . we shall not flag nor fail. We shall go on to the end. We shall fight in France, we shall fight in the seas and oceans . . . We shall defend our island whatever the cost may be. We shall fight on the beaches, we shall fight on the landing-grounds, we shall fight in the fields and in the streets, we shall fight in the hills . . . we shall *never* surrender . . . and even if, which I do not for a moment believe, this island or a large part of it were subjugated or starving, then our Empire beyond the seas . . . would carry on the struggle . . . until in God's good time, the New World, with all its power and might, steps forth to the rescue of the Old . . . .

"Let us therefore brace ourselves that, if the British Empire and its Commonwealth last for a thousand years, man will say, 'This was their finest hour'!

"You ask, what is our aim? I can answer in one word: Victory—victory at all costs, victory in spite of all terror, victory however long and hard the road may be; for without victory, there is no survival . . . . "

"Oh, shut up! Shut up!" Catriona said, and went on with her digging. "A baby might be crying!"